THAT JOYOUS ADVENTURE

BY

E. E. COWPER

AUTHOR OF "GIRLS ON THE GOLD TRAIL"
ETC.

THOMAS NELSON AND SONS, LTD.
LONDON, EDINBURGH, NEW YORK
TORONTO, AND PARIS

CONTENTS

THAT JOYOUS ADVENTURE

CHAPTER I

"WHAT IS IT?"

"Miss Di! Miss Di!" called a shrill and rather queer-toned voice, "come on in; your supper's ready." There was something urgent in the demand—more than was justified, perhaps, seeing that the aforesaid supper was placed on a hot-water plate beneath a shining cover, therefore would not get cold till the water did.

Diana Lindsay, standing alone on the desolate wooded shore that bordered a creek on Blacksand, listened to the call as she gazed out over the rippled surface of Blacksand Water and wished she was at home in a certain vicarage in the Midlands, where her parents worked hard for an expensive family, and went without all the pleasant things of life.

The Lindsay family was expensive because there were four boys at school to start in life. Diana was the only girl; she was sixteen, half-way down the list—two boys above, two boys below! Holidays were usually perfection, but this year there had been a severe outbreak of measles at Diana's school, so she was not allowed to go home and infect her brothers.

Instead she was "boarded out" with Emily Wessel, sometime house-parlourmaid to the Lindsay family, and now married to Job Wessel, sheep farmer, of the farm Tharp Ash, on Blacksand Water.

Low, flat country on the east coast, with spread after spread of shining inland waters—Blacksand, Crowsand, Watergates—channels cutting through from one to another, and queer little villages set on the shores among boats, quays made of ancient piles, brushwood, and poplar trees chiefly.

At the back of Blacksand was Vange Moor, wide-spreading, lonely flats, and thereabouts was Crow's Market, a fair-sized town with long quays built on one of the rivers. Over miles of flat lands, marshes, and waters lay the open sea. The scent of it and its fresh strength blew over everywhere, and made these rather lonely, rather marshy flat tracks sweet and healthy.

Diana had been some few days at Tharp Ash, and already her white face had taken on a new look. Diana's face was white, not so much from measles as from despondency because the boys were far away and the whole summer holidays were to be spent here, alone, in the care of Emily Wessel, with very little to do and less to read. Moreover, Diana did not care much for Mr. Wessel, who was in no way her ideal of a farmer. On the contrary, he was short, wiry, and rather bow-legged, much more like an ill-tempered groom than a nice, stout sheep farmer. Diana had decided that he "nagged" at Emily, who was very tall and very plain, with a forehead that shone from much yellow soap, and a nose so small that it was of no account in her round face.

" Do come on in, Miss Di," said the voice of Emily Wessel from within the broken-down fence that divided the garden from the dreary creek banks.

Emily's voice sounded anxious and fretful, therefore Diana thought she was worried about her young lodger—worried about the mist, the damp, and the oncoming evening. Thinking that, the girl was sorry for her. She need not have been, for Mrs. Wessel's anxiety was about other matters.

" I shall come out again presently, Emily," warned Diana, looking at the farmhouse as they went up the brick path.

" Oh, I wouldn't if I was you, missie, 'deed I wouldn't. It's damp on the water's edge. Now look here. I'll light a little bit of fire in your room ; you have a nice book, or write a letter to your Ma. You keep indoors to-night ; there ain't nothing to be gained by getting about down there on the Blacksand creek."

Diana said nothing. The Wessels did not possess books ; she had written to her mother earlier in the day. For some unexplained reason she was filled with a keen desire to go out along the edge of the creek to the point from which she could see Blacksand Water in the moonlight. A day or two before—to be exact, the evening of the day she came—she had seen something that excited her lonely soul to keen interest. Every day she had watched, but had not seen it again. She felt she must try to-night, but had no intention at all of arguing the matter with Emily Wessel. What she did she would do on her own responsibility.

Now Tharp Ash Farm was a very old house, the front covered with overlapping tiles, and the roof to match; the front door opened into a very big living-room with a brick floor; at the back, under a long, down-sloping lap of roof, was a kitchen, a scullery, and a dairy all in a line with back doors opening into a yard and kitchen garden.

To the right of the big centre room was a slice of a room, as it were, intended for a parlour; it had a window in the front, and a little window at the side looking into an untidy shrubbery. This wall, you understand, was the end of the house. The room was rather deep from front to back, but very narrow. It possessed a little fireplace exactly opposite that side window, and over the fireplace was a strip of mirror in a dingy gilt frame, and various large, shiny shells.

At the back of the room a wee stair, cut off by a door, mounted to the bedroom above—to that one little strip of a bedroom. You will see by this description that Diana had, as it were, a little dwelling to herself. Opening from the big living-room was another stair which led to three bedrooms in a row, all looking front-ways, and all leading one into another. These were inhabited by the Wessels, parents and sons, who worked on the farm; daughters were away in service.

Now the hour was half-past seven, therefore daylight, early in August, but a dull and cloudy daylight with small promise of a gorgeous sunset such as glowed oftentimes across these inland waters, turning them into sheets of golden glory.

Diana thanked Emily Wessel for the tiny crackling fire that presently jumped up the narrow little chimney, took her seat by the little round table, and started on the nice pile of buttered egg and minced ham that lay

(3,095)

beneath the shining cover. It was good ; so also was the home-made bread and butter, and the cocoa made with newest milk. Emily was a good cook.

" You'd oughter get a scrap stouter, Miss Di," suggested Emily. " You're too thin. I'll bring you a cup of milk before you go to bed."

" Oh *no*, thanks—I hate fat people," said Diana hurriedly.

" Growing young girls is different," answered Mrs. Wessel with some reason. " I want to see you do us a credit time you leaves."

Diana made polite remarks about her health ; she did not want the company of Mrs. Wessel at the moment. There was a feeling of expectation in her mind. Some of us know that feeling—" something is going to happen." She had felt it just now on the shore when Emily came and interrupted her dreams. She was waiting and listening without realizing why, and it was all founded on the thing she had seen—once.

" Don't bother about milk," urged Diana ; " or if you really *wish* to, Emily, do you mind bringing it at half-past eight ? It's no good sitting up burning lamp oil for nothing, is it ? "

Diana felt extremely insincere when she said that, yet it was strictly true. She wanted the milk at eight-thirty to give Mrs. Wessel the impression that it would be her bedtime, yet all the time her heart was thumping with little quick beats of excitement because she knew perfectly well that she did not mean to go to bed, though—here was the oddest part—she was not the least certain what she did intend to do. Something was pulling at her mind and urging her to go and see to something important. What was it ?

(3,095) 2

"Don't make a big fire, Emily dear," said Diana, as she drank the last of the cocoa. "It will last quite as long as I want it. How sweet it looks! I do love a fire."

They talked about the price of coal, while Mrs. Wessel piled the plates on a tray. Diana was not the least interested in the price of coal here, though she knew all about it at home, and sympathized warmly with her mother's cares. The fact was she wanted to get rid of Emily and think, also listen; she was sure there was something she ought to hear, only what could it be?

Diana sat before the gay fire and stared at the flames.

Mrs. Wessel looked at the girl's face and wondered if there was anything more she could do to "fatten her up," for Diana was very slim and very pale; her large brown eyes looked unnaturally attentive in the white setting. She was very pretty and very refined, with delicate black eyebrows and a wide, low forehead. The Lindsays were a very good-looking family; the one girl had all the strong points, with a large share of brains also. Like most brown-eyed people, Diana Lindsay was also something of a psychic—that is, she possessed that sense which seems to warn a person of events they can neither see nor hear. Something happening, or something going to happen!

As Mrs. Wessel went out with the tray Diana was feeling in herself that she did not much *like* Tharp Ash. She liked Emily Wessel well enough, but this queer instinct seemed to be warning her that even Emily Wessel was not quite what she had been in old days.

"There is something at the *back* of it all," thought Diana. "Mr. Wessel has got rather a mean face, and he doesn't look like a farmer—at least one's idea of a farmer. And they don't keep a dog that matters! Now, who ever heard of a farm in such a lonely place with a dog too old to bite! It's not reasonable."

Her thoughts were like that, but perhaps not so definite. Questionings and uneasiness kept on waking up, going to sleep again, yet always waking up.

Mrs. Wessel put down the tray on the table in the large living-room, then she stood still considering, picked up an unused spoon, fork, and various small oddments, carried them to a cupboard, and stood still again. Obviously she, too, was listening.

The scullery door opened and a head was pushed through.

"Well?" questioned Mrs. Wessel.

The head belonged to Mr. Wessel.

"Shouldn't be surprised," said the farmer.

"Must say I wish it wasn't just now," remarked his wife rather fretfully.

"Emily, you're making mountains of mole-heaps," declared Mr. Wessel. "What could be simpler? That's what I say. One gal more or less can't make no manner of difference."

"One *gal*!" echoed Mrs. Wessel in a hissing whisper. "An' what about the *Gadfly*? You don't seem to consider *she* can sting—an' then where'll we all be?"

CHAPTER II

DIANA IS IMPELLED TO ACT STRANGELY

DIANA sat in the armchair with the broken springs—quite comfortable it was owing to the hole in the middle of the faded seat. She sat with her feet towards the well-polished fender and back to the window in the *end* wall—that is to say, the end of the house that looked out upon the drear, scrubby bit of copse and brushwood. Over the front window she had pulled the little curtain, and the reason that made her pull the curtain over the window overlooking the front garden, yet not over the window that overlooked the copse, might have been hard to explain. It was just one of Diana Lindsay's queer " feelings."

At half-past eight Mrs. Wessel came in with a thick tumbler full of warm milk and some biscuits on a tray. She set down the tray, walked to the uncovered window and drew the curtain, then she said—

" That all, missie ? "

" Yes, thank you very much, Emily," answered Diana, yawning rather obviously. " I do hope it will be fine to-morrow ; I want to bathe." She flipped over the leaves of the battered magazine she held in a lazy manner.

" I expect you'll soon be in bed, missie ? " ventured Mrs. Wessel, glancing round the narrow room in rather an uncertain manner.

" Probably," allowed Di ; " but a fire is jolly good company. I love fires. By the way, I'll put the guard on safely. One has to be careful, especially in very old houses."

" Thank you, missie," and Emily departed in the secretive manner that seemed to have become habitual to her since she married Mr. Wessel.

Diana read for about ten minutes, then she sat up and looked round at the covered window in the end wall. Then she got up and peeped behind the curtain. Twilight, but not night.

" Nothing could happen till it is really dark," thought the girl, but she opened the window and listened intently.

While the casement was open she measured the frame, and, stretching out, looked at the height from the ground outside. Nothing to be afraid of, certainly. She closed the window again softly, drew the curtain, and sat down in the crippled chair.

From the living-room next door came a sound of low voices—growling remarks from Mr. Wessel no doubt, peevish answers from Mrs. Wessel. It seemed that no one else was in the house, neither of the sons, who were grown up and stepsons to Emily Wessel.

Diana assumed that poor Emily was cross because the two sons, Job and Stanley, would want supper all over again presently.

" Can't think why she married that horrid little Wessel," thought Di, staring at the fire. " She was much happier when she lived with us. Her work is never done here at Tharp Ash. She doesn't look nearly so happy."

Presently the subject of these opinions came in again.

"You goin' up to bed now, missie? I wouldn't sit up if I was you," said Emily.

"Oh, I shan't," Diana told her. "Shall you see to the fire, though?"

Diana wanted to understand whether Mrs. Wessel proposed to come back to the little sitting-room or no, but Mrs. Wessel would not commit herself—"she daresayed it was like enough," and went.

So the girl put on the fire-guard and went up to her bedroom, which was exactly above the lower room in size and arrangement, even to the position of the windows. Then she took off her shoes and dress, slipped on her nightgown, and got into bed.

There she lay listening and thinking, the burden of her thoughts being "I *wish* she would, but why should she? She may not take the least interest in me, of course, but she saw me more than once—I saw her looking—but why didn't she come and call? Why *not*? She's alone and I'm alone; we might have a divine time together, only these idiot Wessels don't seem to want me to speak to a human being. Why? *Why?* Emily says Mummy wouldn't wish it. Utter bosh! Mummy wouldn't mind if I found a decent girl to talk to, and she wouldn't mind one scrap if I——"

Here came a check to the flow, because the thinker was aware of a little sound, a very little noise like tapping and scraping somewhere close by. After listening intently for fully a minute, Diana slid out of bed and went to the window in the end wall—it was exactly over the similar window in the room below. The girl put her head out very gently and searched the copse with eager eyes. Not easy to see now, because night had closed in and the moon not yet risen; trees and brushwood had shaped themselves into uncanny outlines.

Diana gazed eagerly trying to define, and it was then she heard again a quick little tapping like a summons, so close that it made her jump. She had been looking out too far; now she looked *down*, and saw a black figure immediately beneath and outside the little window of her sitting-room. Leaning out she could discern the firelight jumping on the thin little shade of the curtain, but no one could see through.

Diana considered how to attract attention. She dare not whistle, a whistle has such a clear sound. Only a moment she hesitated; then she imitated the sleepy chirruping sound of a disturbed bird roosting. There were few nature noises that she and her brothers did not use in an emergency. At the same time she picked up the biscuit she had brought upstairs but not eaten, broke a bit off, and dropped it with good aim on the *head* below.

A white patch appeared in the dusk as a face was turned upward.

" I want to speak to you," breathed a voice.

" I guess she can see my head and my short hair," thought Diana, " or she wouldn't risk speech." Aloud she whispered through her hands, shaped funnel-wise: " I will drop a note."

Then diving back into her room she seized a pencil from her dressing-table, tore off half a sheet of paper, and wrote by the light of her torch—

" Am waiting till Mrs. W. has been to look at the fire. Then will come down. She thinks I am in bed."

Having written, Diana looked round for something

heavy enough to make the drop sure, saw nothing suitable, so she deliberately tied it to her shoe by the lace, and dropped it down on the girl below.

She watched and saw the other catch the shoe, find the note and read it by her own flash-light, crouched against the wall. Then up came the whisper—

"Right—I'll wait."

Only just in time, for Diana heard Emily in the room below.

Without hesitation she slipped back into bed, drew up the sheet and shut her eyes. Listening intently, she heard the door at the foot of the little stair creak and open. With cautious pauses and suspicious hesitations Emily Wessel came upstairs, and, of course, her coming made all the uneasy little noises that people always do make when they try hard not to.

Diana, hearing it all, thought to herself—

"And why on earth is she like this? She's a perfectly new person—not in the least like the Emily who was so jolly at home! What can she be up to? There *must* be something."

Then she ceased to think, and simply followed the movements of Mrs. Wessel about the room in her mind. Frankly, it was not at all pleasant. Moreover, there are few things more unpleasant than to lie with shut eyes doing your level best to appear profoundly asleep while somebody comes and stares at you!

Diana could not stand it for long. She twisted round, opened her big dark eyes, stared vaguely, and asked in a confused voice—

"Who is it? What's the matter?" Then in a more natural manner, and with rather an offended air, "Emily! What *do* you want?"

Mrs. Wessel looked and was uncomfortable, for she had been trying to see if the girl was really asleep.

"I do wish you wouldn't," said Diana irritably. "I don't call it good manners to come staring at people like that. I was just comfortable."

Mrs. Wessel several times said she was sorry. She was confused at being caught, especially as she had not been able to make certain of her object.

"Don't drop candle grease over all my things, please," said Diana sharply, rising on her elbow, "and see that the fire is out, and after that don't come and wake me again. I loathe being peeped at by creeping people. I shall lock my door inside if you are going to do that sort of thing."

Mrs. Wessel went, rather cowed: she was that kind of person, which was no doubt why she gave in to Mr. Wessel when she had better have been standing on her own principles.

"Poor Emily," thought Diana. She had always liked Emily, yet nowadays there was something oddly irritating about her manner.

"It's enough to *make* a perfectly harmless person do things," muttered the girl, sitting up in bed. "One is not in the habit of *wanting* to go to bed in a sly manner—with half my clothes under my nightie; nor do I make a practice of getting out of windows to confer with girls I don't know about things that are no business of mine. But still, in *this* case——"

That was it: what was this case, and why was she drawn by a sort of irresistible instinct impulse into this business?

She heard Mrs. Wessel dealing with the fire, and finally retreating to her own part of the house. She waited ten minutes or so, then she got up and looked out of the window, chirruping once again in the sleepy note that one often hears in the woods. A white patch showed as a face was again turned up. The strange girl was waiting down there beneath the wall. Diana began to feel rather a thrill of excitement.

She got ready in quick time, and went downstairs cat-like, holding her one shoe. A dim glow came from the red-hot cinders of the raked-out fire inside. Outside was silence.

Diana went to the window, put her head inside the curtain, opened the casement, and chirruped softly.

Instantly she heard a soft rustle, the snap of dead twigs, and was face to face with some one whose head and shoulders just reached above the window ledge.

" Come out," urged a low voice. " You can get through, can't you ? I want you outside."

" Right-o. Got my shoe, by the way ? " asked Diana.

" I have. Guess you got the other. This is simply great getting you. I did so hope I could make you understand."

" There was a good deal of telepathy about it all through," whispered Di as she slid over the window frame feet first. " Shoe, please."

CHAPTER III

ENTER AN INTERESTING PERSON

" FOLLOW me, and be as quiet as you can," said the strange girl, " we can't talk here." That was spoken in a whisper as Diana tied her shoe. Then she, the stranger, went off like a shadow, and Diana followed, trying to pick her way among dead twigs and interfering bushes, for it was dark now ; as yet no moon, too.

The leader made a circuit through scrubby growth of alders, thorn, willows, and the untidy undergrowth that covered these low shores in a rank kind of fashion. Diana, who possessed a good bump of locality, felt that they were going round the farm and making for the coast on the other side. When they crossed a cart-track she supposed it came from the village of Watergate, and tried to see where it led to.

She noticed at this point that her companion bolted over the road like a frightened rabbit, and wondered what there was to be afraid of anyway. As the other girl paused in hesitating fashion, Diana went up to her and asked in a low voice where they were going. The answer startled her.

" Be quiet, for any sake. We must make sure there is no one in the way—they're all over the place just now. Hark ! "

Di shrank into herself, feeling snubbed. It seemed

as though this girl she had been so anxious to know was slightly demented at any rate! A faint qualm about her own position awakened. It seemed so idiotic to be plunging about in a wet wood with a girl whose name she did not know, and to have reached the situation by climbing out of a window! "One hates behaving like a silly ass," passed through Di's mind: also, she disliked being snubbed.

Then she felt a small, strong hand grip her arm and she was pulled down into the black shadow of an alder clump. On that instant she realized the passing of a bicycle along the track from the farm, and, oddly enough, the thing that struck Diana most forcibly was that this bicycle, ridden at a great pace, had no lights —neither the front or back lamps were lighted. From where they crouched they saw it pass against the faint skyline.

"*No* lights," she whispered indignantly.

The other girl gave the slightest chuckle.

"Did you see which of them it was?" she asked.

"How do you mean?"

"Was it Job or Stanley Wessel, I meant. They're all in it, of course. He must have gone to give notice the coast is clear for the car lorry. Come on, now, we shall be just in the very nick."

Diana thought "nick" of what? but asked no questions, and followed as lightly as it was possible to step. Down they went, and down into deeper shadows and more tangles. They had to be careful not to catch a hasty foot in one of the many roots. Then suddenly, by the faint sound of lapping and the shine of pale-grey shimmers, Diana knew they were on the edge of water.

Silently her guide drew in a boat close—so close that the gunwale brushed furtively on the twigs and leaves of the willows.

" Get in," came a whisper, " the sail is down. Any seat—doesn't matter. I shall scull her out presently and then get the sail up ; but that depends——"

She did not say *what* anything depended on ; but Diana was getting used to complete mystery, and accepted the situation. Vaguely she supposed that the boat was very large. As a matter of fact it was about twelve feet—that seems large when you are not used to boats. It was more or less half-decked, with a seat round the open well in the stern, narrow, pointed bows finished by a smart little bowsprit, and a graceful duck stern.

Diana stepped down with a feeling of high adventure ; then she stooped and peeped in at the cuddy door, drawn by a little glow of red light. At the first glimpse she made out a low seat on one side, a bunk on the other, a fixed table, and that the light came from the red glass door of a miniature stove. It occurred to her that there was no stuffiness and no smell of oil ; afterwards she knew that this extremely convenient little stove was electric, and used for cooking. The cuddy was not more than eight feet long, but as Diana realized afterwards it is truly wonderful what you can do with eight feet if you stick to order, method, and possess the natural gift.

" She's twelve foot on the water-line, but over the counter rather more, of course. Right at the end, in the cupboard, I keep stores—in the stern is the water-keg. That little pole down the middle behind the stove is the mast. I can lift that out when I want.

She's absolutely top-hole for safety and convenience," said the strange girl with obvious pride. "Only thing on earth I miss is an engine; but we haven't room for that. Some day when Dad makes a pile he'll give me a motor boat for a change: meanwhile there's nothing about these waters to match the *Gadfly*."

"Oh, *this* is the *Gadfly*," murmured Diana.

"Who told you about her?" asked the other, sitting down on the narrow bed and staring across at her capture who was on the seat opposite.

"Nobody *told* me anything about anything; but I'm sure I heard the name since I came—when the Wessels were talking. I heard old Wessel say to his sons, 'Seen the *Gadfly* about?' That was yesterday."

"You might have seen her name on the bows," suggested the other.

Diana shook her head.

"Too far off. But I saw you several times and wondered who you were, and adored your boat, and admired the way you sailed also. Naturally I wanted to know much more, because Mrs. Wessel was always trying to get me away when I was interested. I could see with half an eye that they didn't *want* us to meet."

"That's interesting," said the other; "but I don't want to wake them too soon."

"Wake them from what?"

"From security, my dear girl. They've been raking in the shekels this last year without any interference. Now it is dawning on their thick intelligence that some one is not quite asleep; but I don't want them to be clever too soon."

There followed about a minute of dead silence, no sound but the ripple of water as it hurried past the sharp bows of the *Gadfly* and washed her sides. Then Diana took her courage in her hands and said what she had been aching to say.

She had been watching the face of this queer stranger ever since she got used to the pink glow of the stove light, and she had come to the conclusion that the owner of this boat was not in the least like any one she had met before, and was well worth knowing.

"Look here," she began, "I don't know whether you know who and what I *am*, but I haven't a notion to whom I owe this joyful adventure. I saw you on the water, and I heard mention of your boat as the *Gadfly*. I wanted to speak to you, but never seemed to hit off the time you landed. As I said before, Emily Wessel seemed to call me in or interrupt whenever I had the ghost of a chance of making your acquaintance. She did to-day. I saw she did not want me to ask you here; but for one reason or another I couldn't get you out of my head. My name is Diana Mary Lindsay. My father is a vicar who works himself to a shred—my parents together are the most adorable people ever invented. I'm the only girl, but there are four boys, Tom and Pelham, older than I, Dan and Spenser younger, and I'm sixteen and a half. The difficulty of educating and starting in life four boys is simply appalling, so as soon as I can I'm going to get a job. That's the whole story—oh, except that we got measles in the summer term this year at my school. I had it, so couldn't go home to Malford—that's our village—Malford and Eastbridge, on the edge of Cambridgeshire, is Dad's job. So they asked Emily Wessel, who used to be our housemaid, to have me here for a month—you see the boys had to be considered. Lodgings are deadly expensive this time of year especially, and poor Emily was awfully pleased to have me for a pound a week all told. She used to be a dear, but something has happened. She's quite a different person, and she doesn't look happy either—at least not my idea of happiness."

"I can call you Diana, I suppose," suggested the other girl in a voice that was rather deep and very clear. "I like your name; I like your—your story awfully. In a minute I'll show you that we're in the same box after a fashion; that is as far as poorness goes. We are newish here; my father is the doctor for all this district—miles of it—my mother is an invalid. We came here for her to get this air, which is perfectly sweet. Dad is desperately clever, but he persists in looking after all the people for nothing, because most of them are on their beam ends—I mean poor gentry who come into little houses hereabouts because it's not fashionable, and they all have sixpence a week to live on—you know the kind! They grow chickens and fruit—and exist. Mostly oldish and faded. Our name is Hamilton, and my name is Noreen Griselda—we are Irish Hamiltons, which accounts for my red hair and Dad's absence of practical method. All the same I wouldn't change him, he's an amazing person. He can do anything and everything, and he sympathizes entirely with my sailing and my aims about motor boats."

"Does your mother mind, though?" asked Diana anxiously.

"Oh *no*! She understands that girls must have something, and I'd far rather do this than parties and all that silly rot. I fish too. I do lots of house jobs—we live in Garde, that awfully quaint village about two miles along the shore, right up a long creek this side of Vange Moor. We've got a dear little house and an old Irish servant called Mary Moore, and that's the whole story, except that I'm seventeen—did I tell you how old I am? No, well, I'm just a bit older than you are, eighteen in November. Filthy month to be born in, and why a person born in November should be a sailor by nature I cannot think: if I'd only been a boy I should have been a middy by now! Diana, just think——"

"I do think," broke in Diana, who had been watching intently the vivid, clean-cut face of this new friend, and noting every point from the tossed back dark red hair to the sharp chin and rather wide, humorous mouth. Noreen was not so pretty as Diana, but she was amazingly attractive and unusual. "I *do* think, and I admire enormously your sailing your boat, and your way of making life exciting. But you have not told me what we are supposed to be doing—*why* we are meeting in the middle of the night and——"

She checked herself because of Noreen's expression and listening attitude, with head on one side.

"Hallo!" murmured she, "hush for your life. I'm going to lock ourselves in, don't move." Dexterously she slid the door of the cuddy along its neat groove—noiseless and water-tight, locking it as it fitted into place. "Now then," she said, "'Quoth the elephant, what next?' That's what *I* say."

CHAPTER IV

IN THE HANDS OF THE ENEMY

DIANA looked round with a disturbed feeling.

Noreen guessed it, for she said—

"You won't be suffocated—ventilator is open, which also enables us to hear what the crowd say. Also, by the way, it's not the middle of the night; it's not eleven yet. Keep your ears open, and I guess this business will explain itself all right; but there is one part I'll break to you later—something we two are going in for—fifty-fifty—as the men say out West. It's purely my idea, and I'm sure you'll agree. Here they come. Now you hush, and just add two and two in silence."

No need to tell Diana to "hush." She was so petrified with amazement that she sat like an image while the sound of a boat scraping along the *Gadfly's* beam was not only heard, but felt.

"*Mind* my paint, you *gardeners*," hissed Noreen, and Diana stared across at her with big brown eyes looking like those of a startled fawn. Why did Noreen call these mysterious prowlers "gardeners"?

A minute after footsteps pattered about on the deck. Then some one stepped down into the steering well and tried to move the door.

"Locked, key gone," said a man's voice. "What will us do, mate—bust it up?"

"*Bust* it, you silly josser! And why for get the perlice on your track, hey? Don't yer know bustin' up yachts is burglary? An' there ain't nothin' to gain neither. This yer boat's the property of that little red-head spitfire, the doctor's daughter."

At this point Noreen shook her fist at the sound and made a face at Diana, who was tempted to laugh.

"Well, what you come aboard for?" demanded the other gruffly.

"See what there is to see, first place—what folks call re-connoitre. Second, to make fast and get this craft out of the way—we want to bring the launch in here; don't you know it's more or less nearest place to Wessel's store? Young Stanley says his ma's got a lodger, and she's scared to death of us bringing things along to the barn as usual. Thinks we'll be overheard. I dunno. What's one lodger in a wide country like this? Why, there's nobody about in miles."

"If you're so sure," said the other in a mocking tone, "what for do you worry about this yer boat? She's a smart little craft—wouldn't mind owning her myself, comes to that."

"Wouldn't you?" snapped Noreen, with such an expression of fury on her sharp little pointed face that Di had difficulty in controlling her impulse to giggle.

However, the next procedure was hardly a matter for giggling. Sounds from the deck above reached their ears. Noreen understood, but Diana did not, though even her ignorance realized in a few minutes that the *Gadfly* was *moving*. No voice came to their ears, by which the fact that only *one* man was left on board presently became obvious.

Noreen knew that her craft was in tow of another boat, and that the one man left on board was steering.

What were they going to do? A boat was straining on ahead, the oars muffled. That was discernible from the soft dull thud that accompanied each stroke. Getting the yacht under way was a stiff pull, but once started she slid through the water with easy motion. Diana sat looking at the owner, whose shape she could just make out by the dim greyness that entered through the glass along the strip of deck-house that rose above the deck. You could not see through that glass, of course—it was thick and opaque; but it served two purposes—to make the roof of the cuddy higher in the middle, and to let enough light through to see by in the daytime supposing the door was shut.

The next thing that happened was more than Noreen bargained for, as Diana instantly realized when she saw the girl clench her fist and bring it down sharply on the bed at her side.

The *Gadfly* seemed to be simply floating without forward movement, rocking a little with the shift of the tide. There followed faint sounds of bumping oars and the rattling that seems always to go with boats.

"You're making noise enough to draw the whole coast," complained the man with a gruff voice, whispering huskily.

"Do it yourself then," retorted the other; "a man's got to make her safe, eh? You don't want the dinghy adrift, do you?"

Diana slid across by the table and sat down on the bed.

"What are they doing?" she asked under her breath.

Noreen shook her head.

"I'll pay them out," she hissed vindictively. "How dare they tow my *Gadfly* all over the place! They'll be sorry later."

Diana could feel her trembling with anger. For herself she was still inclined to laugh, though there were all sorts of questions tied up in this business—the first one being how to get home, and how to explain matters to Emily Wessel.

However, all that must be left to fate.

"'Sufficient unto the day is the evil thereof,'" murmured Di.

"What did you say?" asked Noreen.

"Oh, nothing. We——"

But at that moment there was a new development!

The *Gadfly* seemed to spring to life and shiver through all her graceful length. At the same time a rapid, monotonous rattle drummed on the silence. Faster and faster it worked, and the little cutter began to streak through the water, cutting her way at a rapid pace on an even keel.

"How *abominable*," jerked out Noreen, seizing Diana's wrist. "Do you realize? Do you hear? They are towing us behind the motor launch."

"Where?" asked Diana, hardly appreciating the importance of events.

"Where? My dear girl, goodness knows where. Out to sea, probably; then they'll leave us adrift to be wrecked, don't you see? No one can bring it home to them; people might think she had dragged her anchor and gone adrift! Idiots might. Naturally she couldn't do that in a calm night. But no one could fix it on *them*. The absolute beasts!"

Diana opened her eyes at the concentrated bitterness of that " beasts." She thought boats were delightful things, but it was beyond her power to understand Noreen's devoted love for her *Gadfly*, or her fury at the disrespect shown to the pretty craft by these mischievous men. As a matter of fact, Diana was really thinking more about Tharp Ash and what would happen in connection with Mrs. Wessel and herself! No one could deny that it was a puzzling situation.

The *Gadfly* flew through the water in tow of the motor boat. The girls knew that a man steered, because they heard him cough or grunt irritably now and then, but he did not call out to his mate. Noreen lay on the bed and stared at the beams above her. She said she was calculating where they could be going to, so Diana retired to her side and lay on the seat listening, but not calculating anything except time!

Presently they slowed down, and the busy " chugging " of the launch ceased. Then, from somewhere higher up yet fairly close came a voice, apparently asking questions, which were answered by the motor man. Then some one laughed. Noreen rose to her knees, and bringing her eyes quite close to the glass panel, tried to see what was happening. She gathered some idea, because she crept over to Diana and whispered—

" I believe we are alongside the steamer."

" *Steamer!* Whose? "

" Oh, the men bring one in and anchor her out in Crowsand. Then, you see, they shift the things. But she doesn't come in very close any time, because the tide might leave her on the mud and make it awkward."

"Oh," murmured Diana, trying hard to look intelligent, but not succeeding.

She did not like to bother Noreen with questions, yet she was, so far, entirely at sea as to what "things" might be. She could realize that it would be awkward for a "steamer" to stick on mud, but why should such a large vessel come to this place! You see Diana's idea of a "steamer" was an ocean liner, or, at the smallest, a Channel boat with some hundred passengers. She did not realize such vessels as auxiliary steam dredgers, or the staunch little steam craft that work in the fishing fleet.

"Wish I could hear what they say," muttered Noreen restlessly as she went back to her bed.

Then suddenly she gained her wish.

"Herringford's good enough," said the wheezy voice of the man steering the *Gadfly*.

Somebody said something, apparently disputing this, for he went on—

"Well, and what's the matter with Midbrake? Andy Walduck's no early bird: he's one of the easy kind; *he* won't trouble. If she gets on, say, now, tide'll leave her dry on the mud till long after we've cleaned out. Here you, Kearns, if you don't make up your mind pretty sharp we'll miss the lorry and get stranded. You're not so clever as you think you are."

Growlings and grumblings followed. Finally the *Gadfly* slid on her way pursued by shoutings from a voice on the anchored vessel—very subdued shoutings, of course.

"I can pretty well guess where we shall find ourselves, *dash* it all," raged Noreen. "And what on earth——" she collapsed in mutterings.

It might have been ten minutes before the thing happened that she expected.

Diana, meanwhile, was holding her breath as she waited for some violent bump and a heel over. She was picturing the *Gadfly* on some barren shore, a dreary coast strewn with rocks, and the lovely little cutter a plaything of fierce waves. All that. And then she suddenly felt oppressed by *silence*—the chugging of the fussy motor boat had grown fainter and ceased. Just for one minute there was a sound of movement in the steering well outside. A step, a few words, a quiver of the hull, then the *Gadfly* had ceased to move. Silence—sleepy silence—and then, some way off this time, the rattle of the motor engine retreating in the distance.

Diana sat up and stared across the cuddy.

"Noreen," she whispered, "what's happened?"

"Only they've left us."

"Well, what do *we* do?"

"Not sure till I know where we are."

"But—shan't you look?"

"In a moment; I'm waiting for them to be well out of sight. I think we've got a bit of moon, though. Perhaps——"

Noreen's voice was quite different. She had refused to hope before; now she had waked up into her normal mood.

She opened the door, sliding it back in the silent groove. Instantly Diana put her head out, breathing in the sweet night air in gasps.

"Oh, how *heavenly*!" she sighed.

And really that word seemed to describe the scene, lighted by mist-veiled moonlight. They were in a broad channel fringed by low woods, and the *Gadfly* was drifting very slowly, broadside on, towards one shore, and yet outwards in a direction that suggested wide water.

"Quick, quick, Di—we haven't a moment to lose," urged Noreen. "We must get out before we stick."

CHAPTER V

"GADFLY" LOSES THE FIRST GAME

WITH the faintest of creaks and strains the *Gadfly's* little mainsail went up, and her neat jib flashed out on the bowsprit. She looked like a lovely big moth, and Diana realized how far more conspicuous she would have been with white sails. Her wings were dark red, a lovely warm tint, as she leaned over from the light breeze which seemed to be south-east. There was something so elusive and elfish about her, that Diana felt inclined to cry out with joy. She had never been in a sailing yacht before; rowing boats often, but nothing the least like this—and she found something indescribable in its buoyancy and power.

Noreen was now in her element, entirely wide-awake. Diana sat by her in the stern and watched the clever steering with fascinated eyes.

"Won't they see us when we pass the steamer?" whispered Di in a thrilled voice.

"Not going by that way. I'm sure there is enough water still to take the Midbrake channel back into Blacksand," answered Noreen in an absorbed voice. "I'll risk it, anyway—such a lot at stake. If only we could get back in time to *see* them landing at Tharp Ash. You see, suspicion is no use—we *must* have evidence. Besides——" She was going to say

" Besides, there is you," but became so fixed in the danger of her difficult task that she checked for a minute's pause, then said, " I mustn't talk now. You watch," and fell silent.

The *Gadfly* flew along towards that shining space that looked like open sea, though really the stretch of Crowsand; but instead of running straight across, Noreen swerved down a narrower river channel on the left hand, and letting out the mainsail a little more, they fled before the breeze more than ever like a huge moth flitting between woods.

To Diana it was all like a dream.

The night, with its uncertain silver gleams that showed up weird pictures when the moon broke through the ragged flying clouds—pictures that reminded her of Rackham's " witch " scenes, with their twisted tree-trunks and uncanny creeping roots rising out of wet, muddy banks bared by receding water!

Noreen was absorbed in her work, but Diana sat by with her soft eyes growing bigger as she watched.

" At the end of this Midbrake Water we shall come into old Blacksand," chuckled Noreen. " They won't be expecting us, of course. We shall absolutely *do* them. I'll run in close under Tharp trees again, let the sails down, and we'll go up to the farm and *absolutely* catch them in the very act—you'll see."

" In the act of *what* ? " asked Diana. " About twenty times you've been on the very *tip* of telling me what it's all about, yet I don't know—I haven't a notion. It's really too absurd. Are they burglars, or what ? "

Noreen turned her head and looked at this naïve passenger.

"I didn't realize that! How funny! Not exactly *burglars,* though, of course——" She broke off abruptly, with a faint cry of dismay under her breath, then sprang to her feet, let go the tiller, seized upon a sweep —that is to say, a long oar—that lay along the deck in the scuppers, and thrusting it over the side she began pushing with her whole weight as you would shove a punt on a river.

Diana looked at her, then up at the sails, and realized at once that the *Gadfly* was not moving. The water was rippling along past the slim hull, but the boat herself was simply swerving slowly sideways in the same place. You could see that by the shore.

"Of all the fiendish bits of bad luck!" moaned Noreen, as she pushed hard. "We're *done* simply. Stuck for at least six hours. Tide going out, and we just ran across a mudbank. I *not* attending properly. Oh, what low-down luck! Those inhuman pigs will *see* us lying up on the mud here and simply crow with triumph. Oh *dear*!"

"Can I do anything?" asked Diana, her heart slipping down into a pit of dismay at the thought of Mrs. Wessel calling her, and probably sending off a wire to Mrs. Lindsay at Malford when no girl was to be found in the untidy bed! No girl, no shoes—nothing. Ghastly thought!

"I say, Di, do you mind going forward to the bows? Hold on to the bobstay and just throw your weight off the stern. We are stuck at the stern end, I'm sure. If only we could slip off the bank. *Mud,* you see. That's the worst of it. If only——"

She paused, panting a little, and leaning hard on the sweep.

"She'll never do it," thought Di, her own sense telling her that the long oar would simply sink in and suck them back when she shifted her position; but she stepped along the deck, feeling more sailor-like as she pushed back the enveloping mainsail, flapping across when the boat twisted with the tide.

She reached the forepart of the little vessel, and glancing round to see whether Noreen's position was any more hopeful, her eyes detected something putting off from the shore nearest to them.

She had noticed a wooden hut—just a shelter on the edge of the bank—noticed it vaguely when the moon ray lighted that bit of the wild shore, but now she saw a boat pulling out from the tiny creek on which the shed stood.

Startled at this new situation, she hurried back along the deck, grappled with the bulging sail which threatened to shove her overboard, and hailed Noreen at close quarters.

"Noreen, look! There is a boat coming off from that shed—in the wood—look! Shall we lock ourselves in again?"

Noreen looked, then she pulled the sweep out of the mud and proceeded to wash the blade of the oar.

"Thunderation!" she ejaculated. "I believe it's old what's-his-name! *Not* asleep! Now what will he have to say? Shouldn't be surprised if——"

She stopped short, stared, and nodded.

"Di, he might be a friend, and anyway, having seen us we can't pretend we are not here."

This was obvious, so Diana reconciled herself to the situation, and jumped down into the open part, where she stood by her friend listening to the swift ripple of the tide and the drip of water from the oar blade that stuck out over the counter.

They had not long to wait. A boat was coming towards them at a good pace, but without any sound except that faint, deadened thump that goes with muffled rowing.

"Muffled," whispered Noreen. "And it is old Walduck—he's so fat you can't mistake him."

The boat drew near, and with it came a noise of breathing; there was a pause as it swept round alongside, and a wheezy voice said—

"'Ere, missie, you chuck me a line from your bowsprit. I'll get you off. You ain't bad stuck. Quick as you like; we ain't got no time to lose—tide's sorta racing out."

It was Andy Walduck of Midbrake Farm, the largest, fattest person within miles, and possessing the odd, thin, squeaky voice that seems to go quite often with that style of man.

"I call that kind," said Noreen warmly, as she beamed on the farmer. "But I say, Mr. Walduck, how did you know we were here? We've only just run on this bank."

"An' a good thing too," wheezed Mr. Walduck. "You got a line? That's right. 'Ere, I'll make it fast. I never see you till I happened along. Didn't know you was 'ere. Fact is, I was just moving around on the look-out for them moonlighters, or moon-rakers, whatsoever the books labels on 'em. For all I knowed they might be carting some of the stuff *my* way, and landing me in trouble with them 'Size men—or Customs. Always knows when they come along, an' I got no patience with 'em—a lazy lot, not content to do a day's work and take a day's wage honest. Get-rich-quick job all along the line nowadays. I got no patience."

Growling under his breath, half to himself, the stout Mr. Walduck worked his way along the beam, line in his hands, shifting the boat with his feet. Though he talked and grunted, he did not lose a second, and Diana saw that Noreen was actually dancing up and down on her active toes with joy and excitement.

The next thing that happened was the stalwart rowing of Mr. Walduck. With two stout oars and the whole of his weight he pulled: while it seemed to make no difference, for at every pull the taut line tightened with a jar as though it would snap, and sprays of water flew out from it like a fountain.

Diana went forward. Noreen stuck a pair of tall wooden rowlocks in two holes on the port side of the counter, and slipping her long oar between them, she proceeded to row by pushing the same way you use a paddle in a canoe.

For minutes there was no word spoken—dead silence except for the faint splash of water and the muffled rattle of oars. To Diana it seemed a hopeless struggle, but just as Mr. Walduck paused to take a panting breath, the *Gadfly* made up her mind that she preferred water to mud, and shifted ahead with a little sliding movement.

Noreen muttered, " Three cheers—Brit-ons never—never—nev-er shall be slaves," and started paddling with double force.

Mr. Walduck threw himself into a mighty effort, and a minute after the cutter slipped forward with a definite glide that showed she was free of her dangerous bed. The stout little boat continued to forge ahead under the farmer's efforts, till they were in midstream, then Mr. Walduck let himself drop alongside the *Gadfly*, unrove the line, curled it deftly, and threw it on board.

"You're right now, missie," he said, as he sat down again and wiped his head with a vast handkerchief. "Don't you cut no more corners on the ebb tide, and good-night to you."

Noreen leaned over to shake hands.

"Mr. Walduck, you're a brick—you're a friend in need. Think what you saved me from!"

"Oh ay, I do think—I think more'n a little," chuckled Mr. Walduck. "Good luck to ye," and gripping his sculls he slid away into the shadows of his own shore.

The *Gadfly* bent to the breeze, and they fled away down the centre of Midbrake till they came to Blacksand. Diana did not know it, but Noreen did, and looked out eagerly for the signs of the enemy.

One way and another time had been lost; also, this was a long way round, and when Noreen let down her little peak and slipped into a bushy creek the whole shore seemed to be deserted.

"Oh, how *sickening*," whispered Noreen. "They've *done* us—they've won this time."

Di stared at her, wondering; then she heard and understood. From the land came the sound of a motor car—a lorry—racing away westwards.

CHAPTER VI

THE BOAT-HOUSE

DIANA waked from profound sleep when Mrs. Wessel brought hot water at seven o'clock.

"I think, Emily," she said, shutting her eyes again, "I think I shall bathe later on, when the sun's out. It is so misty now."

"Hope you had a good night, missie," said the farmer's wife.

Diana considered a moment, a little smile flickering round her mouth as recollections of the "good night" flowed back over her mind. She opened her eyes about half-way.

"Well, yes," she answered; "but really, Emily, for a quiet place you do have an awful lot of noise in the night here. There was a motor car, or lorry, quite close, making a beastly row—and I'm *sure* I heard a steam launch too. What is it all about? Why can't your people do their business in the day-time? Much more sensible."

Mrs. Wessel appeared to take on a tint of extra yellow, which stood for pallor in her.

"I wish they would indeed, missie," she answered eagerly. "Them folks sending down hay for one thing; and the master has to hire a cutter for the corn crop too. Often as not they send along them things at night-time to save a day's work."

"Oh, do they? Well, you tell Mr. Wessel it woke me up last night. I'll come and see him using the corn-cutter—it's so interesting to watch."

It was observable that Emily's jaw seemed to drop as she realized this idea.

"Don't you get too close, missie," she urged. "For the life of me I can't get used to them whirling machines —I hate 'em."

"So do I—in the middle of the night," agreed Diana, sitting up in bed with a yawn. "I don't want to get up, Emily, at *all*, but I will have breakfast at eight, because I'm going out for a sail with Miss Hamilton to-day, I hope."

Diana looked at the window. She seemed greatly interested in the weather, as was, of course, very natural. She did not look at Mrs. Wessel, who checked by the door and stood, apparently waiting.

"It will be lovely if it's fine," went on the girl. "I do love boats."

"I wouldn't go out in that *Gadfly* boat, not if I was you, Miss Di," said Mrs. Wessel, finding words. "I didn't know you had acquaintance with Miss Noreen. By all accounts she's a very wild young lady —very. Riskin' her life all over the waters, an' her mamma in very poor health, too."

"I'm sorry to hear that," remarked Diana in a silky voice. "I must say I like her most awfully. And it does one good to go on the water—you get such lovely air."

Mrs. Wessel made sounds of expostulation, but Diana lay down again and gazed at the window. Evidently there was no more to be said, so the farmer's wife departed.

It was then that Di Lindsay really woke to review with feelings of profound amaze the adventures of the past night. She was sleepy, but she was very happy, for never in her life had she experienced anything so interesting. She dwelt in mind over again on every phase up to the final landing on the narrow spit of shore where Noreen anchored the *Gadfly* to the bank, and accompanied her up through the underwood by the farm buildings, to the north end of the house.

It was not till then that Diana was seized with a fear that the window might be shut—latched, in fact! In which case the situation would present difficulties.

Noreen comforted her with a whispered invitation either to Garde or to the cabin on the *Gadfly*.

"All you'd have to do would be to walk in early in the morning and say you had been out! I don't see anything to bother about," said Noreen. She was like that—no difficulty seemed to her a serious matter.

Diana, a different kind of girl, was quite capable of resorting to either of these plans if she was forced to, but even the idea of it was to her rather horrible. She knew she would have felt ashamed of herself when meeting Emily Wessel, and that was a degrading idea. So she hoped with all her heart that Emily had *not* touched the window when she came on that queer scouting expedition the night before, and rejoiced when they found it was so, and all was well. The window was closed but not latched, so that a pen-knife under the edge levered it open.

The girls had parted with promises and plans for sailing and explorings of the waters.

"And above all," whispered Noreen, "you faithfully

promise and vow, my dear girl, that you will help me and back me up right through in this business."

"I promise," said Diana. "I'll be down on our shore to-morrow; I want to bathe about eleven or twelve, and——"

"Can you swim?"

"Not well—only a bit"

"I'll fetch you before eleven, and we'll go towards Garde and bathe from the *Gadfly*. I've got a little ladder. Oh, and I say, Di——"

"I must *not* stay any longer now," urged Diana, "truly not now. I'm in deadly danger of getting caught, and want to go to bed. Tell me things to-morrow."

That was the way it ended. Noreen leaned against the wall, stooping, Diana stepped on her back for one minute, and went through the window with ease—if not grace! All was peace and comfort inside, and almost immediately she was asleep.

The last thing Diana remembered before she slipped into dreamland was that, after all that had happened, she did not know what it was all about, or what people were doing or trying to do, and that, though she had asked Noreen several times, something had always got in the way of the answer. This new and very adventurous friend seemed to take it for granted that everything was obvious!

The rest was sleep till Mrs. Wessel came in, and now here was another day, and the curtain lifting on all sorts of new adventures. Diana noticed one thing while she was eating her breakfast—not once had she felt lonely; not once had she regretted the boys' holidays; not once had she remembered the measles, or the slackness that had gripped her since she had them!

She decided to tell her mother how much better she was, and about this new friend, but nothing—as yet—about this queer atmosphere of mystery and probably danger that seemed to pervade Tharp Ash and the lovely waters that lay around in miles of stillness and shining beauty.

It seemed to Diana that Emily Wessel wore an air of secrecy, though, of course, that might have been imagination, especially as it was in no way *guilty* secrecy, but the sort of *pleased* secrecy in which people veil themselves at Christmas-time when they are hiding presents.

Mrs. Wessel was not a person who could keep up deceptions cleverly. She was really, what she had always seemed to the Lindsay family in the old days, a nice woman. Therefore secrecy sat heavily on her, and Diana was in no way blinded by it, because it stared her in the face. At the same time she wondered what it was.

Between ten and eleven she went to the shore by way of the track she and Noreen had followed the night before, as nearly as could be judged. In her mind were two intentions: the first, to see if any one else had been the same way since; the second, to make a more obvious path, a path well trodden, so that a suspicious person might think it was an habitual track. Afterwards, she was glad she had thought of doing that.

Pressing through the underwood to the shore, she was faced by soft white mist, lying low all over the water and the woods. Looking out over Blacksand, or rather into the fog that covered Blacksand, she saw the tree-tops above it, where the mist was thin, but *on* the water you could see nothing at all. Diana knew about these mists, but had not, so far, experienced one. She stood still wondering about it, for the minute undecided what to do.

Mrs. Wessel would like her to sit indoors, " read a nice book," or " write to your ma "—then her charge would be under her eye, as it were!

But from Diana's point of view there is small joy in being on your own in rather an interesting world unless you do something novel. She was only just out of school, too, so the wish to enjoy holiday was naturally extra strong.

" If it were cold," thought Diana; " but it's simply stuffy-hot—no wind. I shall bathe, as I said I would," and she squeezed the pretty bathing garment and towel tucked under her arm. She was so much better that she felt a strong intention to have her own way, too.

She made her way along the shore in a direction trending away from the farmhouse. She was looking for a little old boat-house, perched on wooden piles, that she had seen and noted at the edge of the water, also bathed from once already; steps down to the shore, which was sandy mud, empty within, and possessing a door. What more could you ask for to use as a bathing hut?

The one day she had bathed was fine and warm; you could see the shore and the wood that clothed it; you could feel Blacksand lake was all your own, too, not like a seaside resort swarming with holiday folk—no one came to this glorious place.

Diana reconnoitred cautiously, and found herself in peace. She went into the hut by the land door that opened into the wood. The second door was at the top of the steps leading down into the water; underneath, the piles supported the floor, and to all appearances boats had been kept there either floating or on the mudbank, for she had noticed iron staples driven into the piles, and to one a rusty chain hanging with a padlock.

There was an extremely happy feeling about undressing in that uncanny bathing-house in the wood. So seldom is it given to people to do pleasant things in weird circumstances. Life is commonplace, and if you bathe you do it in such an ordinary way that there is nothing exciting in it.

But to Diana, alone in this deserted hut on the edge of the still, inland sea, wrapped up in this strange, secret mist, there was a thrill indeed, and she wished the boys were here to appreciate it all with her. The fact that nobody knew she was here added much to the thrill, of course.

The door would not lock, but that was no matter. Once in her bathing-dress she took her clothes, rolled them into a bundle, and, stretching up, put the bundle over on to the loose planks that formed a kind of rough ceiling. It looked as though some person had started finishing off this hut inside, and, to that end, had slipped a few planks across to rest on the side beams. Then, getting tired of the work, left it. The planks remained, and on them Diana put her bundle, because the floor was wet and muddy, while the planks looked clean.

Then she went down the little ladder into the water.

CHAPTER VII

LOST IN STRANGE CIRCUMSTANCES

THERE was something adventurous about bathing in the mist, and Diana enjoyed it at once. The water was warm and she was a good swimmer ; out she went into the wider waters, knowing that the shadowy tree shapes would show her the way back.

That was all right, but when she had dived under a time or two, and come up wiping the water from her eyes, she suddenly realized that she did not feel sure *which* trees of the many grey shapes sketched on the white veil were those that grew round the bathing-hut. This was annoying; but Di was not the least worried—she could always get ashore somewhere in any case. She swam towards the shore—a shore, but not the bit she was looking for. She paddled along the edge in shallow water, found her feet were getting muddy, swam out again to clean them, and saw, not far ahead, a darker shadow on the mist which suggested the presence of her bathing-hut.

So she made for that, feeling it was time to get out of the water, considering measles and her mother's opinion on these matters.

When she came close to the dark shadow she saw that it was no hut, but a dense clump of alders growing along the bank of a tiny creek, an inlet of the Blacksand Water, or else perhaps a small stream filtering down from higher ground. Diana was disappointed. She was still lost, it seemed! The water was a little above her waist here, and for the first time she was conscious of chill in the mist.

Nothing to be done but get under water and explore the shore farther along. The hut was certainly close by. And then just at that moment she heard *oars*—some one rowing in her direction, coming along towards this alder creek apparently.

She was glad, because this might give her a clear hint as to where she was, but the prospect of being caught in the water by Blacksand people was unattractive. Diana felt she would look undignified all alone, and lost on the shore! She would see what the men did and where they went; that would give her a clue. Meanwhile, she turned into the alder creek, and keeping low in the water she moved up to the beginning of the alder clumps, and there, happy in the thought of shelter, she waited, listening.

But the respite was not for long; in about two minutes she got a shock. Growing out of the mist she saw the bows of a small boat, the clinker-built variety, rather broad and squat in shape. Above the boat loomed the shoulders of a man rowing—his back to her, of course—and in another second or two she saw the shape of another man. The two were rowing, and, what is more, were coming straight up this little creek.

"Oh, *dash*," muttered the girl, and promptly she ducked beneath the drooping boughs and crept up close under the shore. Her annoyance was because the boat would not show her the way to the bathing-hut, as she had expected. And what on earth it could want in this narrow little inlet that led nowhere was a perfectly uninteresting mystery. But though she was not a bit interested in this boat, she was bound to wait till the men had passed her in order to get out of the creek.

The rowers came abreast of her hiding-place. Then she heard the cluck of a rowlock as one man shipped his oar.

" Where did you say they put her, Stan ? " he asked.

It was the voice of Job Wessel, the farmer's eldest son.

" Not here—a bit farther up. For the life of me I can't see what's what in this fog. Anyway, I don't know what you want."

" You can't ! Well, you ain't bright if that's the way you see things. Didn't Kearns say anything to you, then ? "

This was Stanley asking, as Diana made out. Both boys had shipped their oars, and the little craft seemed to float in mid-air as the lowered voices came out of the mist close by.

Then Job spoke again—

" It's a queer business, an' no one can tell what'll come of it. While you was gone on the bicycle to tell those chaps the steamer was in, Pawley and Gaunt nabbed that little devil of a *Gadfly*. She was locked up and no one aboard. Gaunt towed her out alongside the steamer, then Kearns made the launch fast to her, and they took her off alongways right across Crowsand up Herringford way. They left her along shore with the tide racing out. She was fair bound to be there about twelve hours. They come along back, and when they just about got warning of the lorry, who should come along but Harsfold in his dinghy from *Morning Star*. 'You look out,' says he, '*Gadfly's* coming along down from Midbrake channel just about full lick.' 'You're asleep,' says Gaunt. 'Why, *Gadfly's* on the mud far side of Crowsand; she's due to stop there till middle day to-morrow.' Well, there was plenty of words, and then it was all settled, because who showed up off Blacksand but *Gadfly* with sail set. The whole lot of them was mute as fishes. Gaunt and Pawley took their dinghy into Tharp creek and told the lorrymen it wasn't safe. So *they* went, empty, of course. What happened to *Gadfly* none of them could say; there wasn't spar or rag of her to be seen later. Kearns got scared, so he ran his load into this gully under the alders, and left the launch. The other chaps took him back to the steamer, and *she* up anchor and ran down to Crowsand."

"Seem to have made a mess of it," commented Stanley with scorn. "What's the plan now, then?"

"Launch will stop where she is till Timothy Chant can come back with the lorry to lift the goods. But we got to get *Gadfly* out of the way, so Dad told me to bring along this yer dinghy from old Barney's yard up at Garde for the young lady to amuse herself with. That's mother's notion. Seems she's taken up with the *Gadfly* and Miss Hamilton. Mother says, 'distract her attention and she'll just be about here, and come in evenings, and *Gadfly* will keep away 'stead of cruising just around these waters all evening time.' Near shave of getting caught last night anyway—we none of us don't understand it yet."

"You show me where the launch is, anyway," suggested the younger brother, " then we'll go and tie up this craft at the boat-house. Supposing the young lady don't incline to this yer dinghy, I don't see you gain much."

Job defended himself sulkily.

" Mother's notion," he said. " She's set on keeping the young lady off the *Gadfly*. She says this will do it, seeing she's so set on boats. *She* made Dad ask old Barney."

Stanley grunted. It was plain he considered Mrs. Wessel's plan a clumsy failure in advance.

" Oh, well, what's the good of talking," he grumbled. " Proof of the pudding's in the eating, so we are told ! I vote it's times we quit dabbling in this yer milk soup ! I'm sick and tired of it. Tim Chant was none too pleased coming down for nothing last night."

Job made a disrespectful remark about Tim Chant.

" He don't often come down Tharp way for nothing," grumbled Job. " The trouble we take getting in these loads is deserving of what *we* make. Why, Chant must be full of money."

" We shan't be full of anything but bad temper unless we hurry up," retorted the younger brother. " Here, come on, let's see where the launch is laid up, and then we'll quit this."

The fog seemed to swallow them. No sound reached Diana, but she had no idea of surrender to chilly circumstances till she had got to the bottom of this affair. So she crept out from beneath the alder boughs and followed the track of the boat, keeping very low in the water as before.

However, in this case she was as nearly as possible caught, because the boat came suddenly out of the mist, the blunt bows driving straight at her. Both men were rowing, so that their backs were towards her, naturally, otherwise she must surely have been seen. Diana dived under, but before she could get away the blade of an oar knocked against her back. There followed an exclamation and a check. She came up a yard or two farther away, panting a little, and just a bit uneasy to hear the brothers arguing again.

"I tell you my oar hit against something under water;" "Well, shove then. I bet a pound there was nothing;" and so on.

She could see the shadow of the boat drifting round over the spot, while both the rowers pushed their blades downward into the mud. To no purpose, of course, as Diana was some yards nearer the opposite bank.

It was the sort of escape to give a shock! A close shave indeed. But Diana was so interested about the launch that she simply went ahead towards the other bank till the shadows of the alder clumps prevailed over the mist, and she found herself touching the wet, hanging leaves.

Sure enough there it was, drawn alongside the bank in close concealment—a long, slim motor boat, painted black or the very darkest blue. The girl gripped the gunwale, and, raising herself by muscular effort, looked inside as well as she was able. She could see what appeared to be engines. She could see closely packed bundles and boxes, and came to the conclusion that the little cabin that filled up the forepart of the slender craft was probably also full of packages. Amidships were the engines, of course.

Diana wanted to climb inside, but there was no time, because her aim of following the young Wessels to the boat-house held. She dare not let them get quite out of hearing, because she was lost just as much, and the idea of creeping about in the water, shrouded by this dense white mist, was becoming distinctly tiresome !

Anyway, she knew now where the launch was, and a very definite conviction formed in her mind at once that the next thing to do was to get hold of Noreen, tell her the discovery, and find out what the skipper of the *Gadfly* proposed in these very odd circumstances.

I expect it will be understood that Diana was extremely *pleased* in spite of the cold, the mist, and the possibility of a chill. Up till the present Noreen had been so completely in the front—leader undisputed ! Now she, Diana, had something to tell that was worth revealing. She had braved a very unusual ordeal, and made a very startling discovery.

Sliding back into the water, she followed the argumentative voices of the Wessel boys with all speed.

CHAPTER VIII

DIANA AND THE "ARROW"

THERE is no doubt about one thing in life being fairly certain. You may get what you plan for and aim at, but that very thing may bring about what you wish to prevent.

It was so with Emily Wessel's fine scheme for providing her young lodger with a boat. Diana had said she loved boats, and wanted to be on board a boat. Therefore, every day and all day since she came to Tharp Ash, Emily Wessel had "nagged" at her mean little husband to hire a boat of manageable size and let Diana use it. Mr. Wessel objected because of the small extra expense, but when the fact of Diana's association with Noreen became obvious, the farmer gave in. It was plain that their young lodger might gain knowledge of the secret business in which the Wessels were interested, and such knowledge would make for exposure and disgrace! He could see that. So, while they thought there was still time to avert this danger, they got the boat—*Arrow*—a stout little clinker-built dinghy nearly as broad as she was long, and far less like an "arrow" than Emily Wessel herself.

However, that is of no importance. What really mattered was that Diana thanked Mrs. Wessel warmly, and said she would use the *Arrow* every day, probably.

She said she had been out bathing and returned to find the boat tied up under the bathing-hut. She was delighted at such a grand surprise, and thought it so kind when told it was for her use.

It seemed there had been a boat belonging to the boys for years; but it was larger, heavier, and in such bad repair that Mr. Wessel had sent it "up to the yard," for fear the lodger should use it and come to harm.

"You'll be all right with the *Arrer*, missie," said Emily. "The boys say as how she's light to handle, so you can do a bit of rowin' and not be beholden to nobody."

"Nobody," of course, meant Noreen. Mrs. Wessel thought she had succeeded beyond her wildest hopes; but, as before suggested, she had only succeeded in making the thing she was afraid of easier for Diana.

The lodger went out that evening after tea with the *Arrow* looking for the *Gadfly* and the *Gadfly's* active skipper. You see, she did not now have to wait for Noreen to come and look for her.

Diana pushed off from the boat-house with a feeling of high adventure. The mist had cleared about two o'clock, and the afternoon had been lovely. She had some tea early, and said she would row up to the village and go to the post office. Emily could make no objection to that, though she wanted to, by the way, and so Diana and the *Arrow* went off eastward together along the flat wooded shores of Blacksand Water.

Diana had once come this way by road walking to the village, but never yet reached it by water, so she felt much interested. Moreover, she loved scenery, so the weird beauty of the place grew upon her daily—

wide waters, deep, far-piercing creeks, rather mysterious channels linked up one great lake with another. It was a country that invited secrets, and Diana thought to herself as her dark eyes scanned the queer desolation of the shores: "All I can say is, if people did not do queer things *here*, they would be positively wanting in romance! You would have to if you lived here. You simply must *do* story-book things, or catch people who do them! Either way, it is frightfully exciting—this place Garde is one mass of romance. I never saw anything like the old houses and the tumble-down quays, and the boats—and—what *luck*!"

The "luck" was the *Gadfly*, riding sleepily in the still pool of water off Garde quay—water that was pink and gold from reflection of the sky. Around were various shabby fishing-boats of small account, and loafing on the quay were various untidy men, also of no account: the whole place simmering in breathless heat—airless, oppressive, lazy heat—enough to take the energy out of any one.

Diana made straight for the *Gadfly*. There was no small boat astern, but she had an inward conviction that Noreen would be on board; why, she could not have explained.

She drew alongside, stood up in her boat, and holding on to the scuppers with care, she looked over.

"Hallo!" hailed a voice from within the cuddy. "I'm not coming off yet—not ready."

"Noreen," said Diana, realizing that her friend must have been put on board by one of the sleepy frequenters of the sleepy quayside. "I say, can I come on board?"

"*Can* you! Hop over, Di. I say, you got a boat? It's old Barney's dinghy, too. How did you get it ? Oh, by the way, let me make fast : see, like this, on the counter rail."

Noreen appeared as she spoke, seized the painter from her friend, and knotted it in place with a swift turn.

" How did you get here ? " asked Diana as she slipped within the cuddy and looked round with a sigh of satisfaction. With that cursory glance she saw a wet towel and drenched wisp of bathing-dress stretched out before the stove.

" How did *you* ? " countered Noreen, adding quickly, " Have some tea, or plums, or chocolates ! Ice I cannot offer. Hot as blazes, isn't it ? and thunder sitting on our heads. In answer to yours, my dear, I swam out for coolness and practice. I told those lazy lubbers on the quay that one of them could fetch me off when I was ready ; but, as a matter of fact, it doesn't matter, because I could easily swim back and dress again at home. I keep clothes at both ends of the journey. It is only the bother that I shirk ; and that is not exactly serious. However, now you have turned out to be the owner of such a smart craft—— By the way, how *did* you get that tub ?—*Arrow*, isn't she ? About as much like an arrow as old Barney himself."

Noreen positively chattered, her red curls standing on end, her keen eyes dancing, and something sparkling through her sharp features and clear, freckled skin. Diana watched her, smiling. She admired and liked this unconventional girl very much, especially the absence of " side " and patronage. Diana hated being patronized by girls a year or so older than herself ; so she recognized with joy that Noreen was the kind you could get on with.

In a lowered tone she told the story of her queer experience in the mist that morning; of the hidden launch, and the reason that the Wessels had been so generous over the boat.

"It's to keep me away from you and the tiresome *Gadfly*," concluded Diana, a little laugh making dimples in her earnest face. "It really does seem hard on poor Emily that the first thing the *Arrow* does is to bring me *to* the *Gadfly*."

"Hum—hum," murmured Noreen, bringing her straight eyebrows down in a line. "Now this is a very exciting situation."

"Yes?" allowed Diana in a questioning tone.

"The thing that strikes me is that the *Gadfly* might lend a hand just here."

"Might she—oh!" Diana looked still more interested.

"You see," went on Noreen after a pause, "I've got an idea—just a tiny shoot—in the deep of my mind. It requires careful attention; but I *think*"—there was a pause again—"you said they did not expect the lorry to come at once and unload that launch, Di?"

Diana shook her head.

"As far as I could gather, they didn't know when the man would come."

"Eat chocolates while I think," said Noreen, and for minutes there was silence.

It was broken by Diana, who, never a slave to chocolates or any other article of consumption unless she happened to be hungry, was not so much eating as thinking. These thoughts made her break silence.

"Noreen," she began anxiously, because she felt

she was interrupting important considerations, "I say, Noreen, do you mind if I ask you something?"

"Ask away," said her friend, waking up.

"Well, you see I don't really know what it is all about! I mean, who are the men, and what's the steamer? Where do the parcels come from, and why on earth are *we* bothering about other folks' business? I cannot quite see why the Wessels do things in the night, or why they want to keep it secret. Besides, if it is burgling or stolen goods, or disgusting wickedness of that kind, why does not the policeman come and stop them? Anyway, it cannot *possibly* be all right and above board, because of the way those men took us and the *Gadfly* away last night, and the bits of talk we heard. They are doing something wrong. You know what it is—I don't. So won't you tell me?"

Noreen's sharp face crinkled into a smile.

"My dear girl, you mean you really did not guess they are smugglers?"

For a moment there was dead silence. Then—

"Oh," murmured Diana in a tone of profound disappointment She sighed. "But, Noreen, I've always thought smugglers were fearfully romantic and brave. I thought they had battles with what's-its-name men, and sailed splendid vessels in the bravest manner possible. Are you sure, though? And why do they do it?"

Noreen proceeded to explain, nibbling chocolates meanwhile.

"It's a question of getting goods from France into England without paying duty. Or, of course, now, the other way round—for instance, getting tea and tobacco into France. Take tea. It's about eight shillings a pound in *France*. If you take a few hundredweight of our tea at half a crown a pound over there, you can rake in a heap of money."

"Eight shillings! Stars!" murmured Diana, who understood housekeeping.

Noreen laughed.

"These men have got that launch stowed full of silk things—stockings, frocks, all sorts. Also watches, scent, and different medicines. Also saccharine—that is *very* expensive over here, and they want tons for jam, of course."

"Oh," commented Diana, rather vaguely. She had not been interested in saccharine so far.

"So you see," went on Noreen, "these men bring over stacks of goods. People buy and make a jolly big profit because they have not paid duty. *Now* you see."

"*Mean* pigs," ejaculated Diana with scorn.

"Yes, I know. It used to be brave perhaps long ago, when they had to fight strong bands of coastguards and Excise men. Now it's different. When they are caught they get fined—*big* fines. Serve them right. My Dad says they are cheating their own country for private gain. Long ago, of course, smugglers might have been romantic: they certainly are not now. It's no more romantic than cheating a person in a shop, *I* think. Or making sham money, and printing false notes. It's all of a piece—just *cheating*. You see, Di, we are jolly near the other country here on this coast, and this coast is also very convenient for hiding and landing boats."

"Why on earth are these men going on so long, though?" demanded Diana; "if other people know, why can they keep on?"

"The people in the villages will not tell. First, because they could not live here if they showed it up. Second, because the men give them all sorts of bribes. You cannot blame them; they are all related or tied up in business—or something. They all pretend like they did in old days; but they are caught in the *end* —always."

"Of course, and we are going to catch them this time," said Diana, sitting up alertly. "Now I really know I am keen; also, I know, now, why poor Emily always has a guilty face. She never had it when she was honest."

CHAPTER IX

NOREEN HAS AN IDEA

AT that moment an ominous roll of thunder passed overhead, so loud and heavy that the little yacht seemed to quiver beneath the jar of it.

" Oh, I never saw any lightning," said Diana ; " but, of course, it has been awfully hot now for days. It is dark, too."

" I saw it, but it was a long way off," Noreen told her. Then she went on speaking in a decisive tone, leaning forward from her side of the little table and fixing her eyes on Diana's rather perturbed face. "This seems to me rather convenient, because it will make the Wessels think you have taken shelter in Garde from the storm. Diana, I want you to take me back with you *now* in your dinghy, and help me shift all the packages out of that launch."

Di made a startled sound and her dark eyes opened. Noreen shook her head.

" The lorry won't come by day, my dear girl," she reasoned. " I can manage a launch all right—Dad taught me to—but we can't run off with it without making a sound, and the chug-chug of an engine would be heard all over the place. I want to shift all those goods on to my *Gadfly*, see ? "

" Oh, stars and stripes ! " murmured Diana.

" They won't be heavy," reasoned Noreen, " we'll get the *Arrow* alongside, lift them in and take them over. We shall leave the motor boat empty."

" But, Noreen, when they find it empty, they will know about us, won't they ? Not that it matters in a sense ; but, well—what about it ? " Diana looked anxious.

" I've been observing things for weeks, Di," answered the other girl, " and I've noticed that two lorries come, at different times—or, anyway, the men are different. I have seen a lorry come down with boxes and cases on it, heavy-looking things. Well, don't you see that those cases might be tea and tobacco ? Supposing a lorry comes down loaded, their plan would naturally be to put those goods on the launch and believe that the Wessels or the motor men had put the launch cargo on the other lorry, or—or somewhere in the farm. They might be surprised, but they could not possibly think of *us*."

" No, I guess not—perhaps," allowed Diana, rather dubiously. " But if you got the things on to the *Gadfly* what would you do with them ? "

" Take them to Crow's Market. It is *the* important town, and it is away on the other side of Crowsand. We could, of course, give them in at the police station, or tell somebody." Noreen checked, then she laughed softly. " I say, Diana, it would simply be a top-hole stunt if the van lorry with the tea came along and loaded up the launch because they found it empty ; and then I went and got away with the British goods as well—launch and all ! I say, what a job ! "

" Too good to be true," said Diana—" those sort of things don't come off. It would be too—too—— Oh ! I *say* ! "

This last exclamation was caused by a crash of thunder that rolled along over the miles of flat fens and waters like heavy artillery. Before the echoes were silent the cuddy was illumined in every detail by the quivering brilliance of more lightning.

"Oh, crikey!" said Noreen, as she sprang to the hatch and looked out. "Up, down, around, land and water!" Then she went up into the steering well with a bound and began hauling on the painter of the *Arrow*.

"Going in *this*! But look here, Noreen——" Diana was out after her instantly.

"Of course, of *course*, my sweet child. Don't you see it is simply a godsend for our plan? Every man, woman, and child has rushed for shelter; if they are not in their houses they are lying flat under their boats. In Garde they weep with terror when they hear thunder. As a matter of fact, it does sound extra loud in this country. All gone, Di. Now we will take your boat, and go back while the coast, literally, is clear."

"But, Noreen, I thought you said we were to load up the *Gadfly*," protested Diana in a breathless whisper.

"Can't get her there, dear child. There is not a shred of breeze. There *will* be when the storm is over—lots of wind. We will come back to her then—and finish. Here, get in—hurry all you know. I'll just lock up the *Gadfly*."

What Diana wanted to know was, what was the good of going if they could not unload the launch! She would not ask Noreen though, as it made her seem foolish, or rather *feel* foolish! Noreen must have a reason. There was something convincing about her shrewd face and vivid personality. If she said a thing must be done Diana felt there was no sense in questioning her—she would do it.

The two girls rowed away in a perfect riot of thunder crashes, and surroundings that were oddly dramatic. The dense clouds overhead were shot with coppery tints and queer colours that looked unnatural. Every minute almost they were split by downward blades of light—of flame that burned blue and seemed to disappear into the still waters. There was not a breath of wind, as Noreen said; every leaf was deadly quiet—even the tide appeared to be held up. The dreary quay was deserted, and Diana noticed that the one or two cottages on the shore, and the little inn that stood back by the roadside, all had their curtains drawn or blinds down. No doubt of one thing—they two girls had the place to themselves for the duration of this storm anyway.

Both rowing, the girls pulled their hardest along the shore. Noreen with the bow oar turned her head to manage the steering, and spoke every now and then.

"Mrs. Wessel won't worry about you, Di—this storm will explain your absence."

Diana jumped as the lightning glimmered into their faces, then she agreed.

"Emily is terrified of thunder. She is probably under her bed now."

"All the better—let her stay there."

Noreen laughed, pulling hard and watching the shore anxiously.

A few minutes after that Diana saw where they were, and questioned for the first time.

"But, Noreen, this is not the alder creek; we have to go a bit farther. This is the——"

"I know. We are going to the boat-house. I'll explain in half a jiff. Here we are—we will run in under the boat-house and tie up. If any one should happen to see us, it is *the* most innocent place to be found in—don't you worry."

Diana did not worry, but she wondered! They ran in by the piles and made fast; got out, crept up the bank and into the boat-house, which was exactly as Diana had left it.

"Now," said Noreen, looking round, and especially at the loose planks of the ceiling, "now, my dear, we will fetch everything we can carry from the launch and bring it here. We can put it up there"—she motioned towards the roof—"and——"

"And if the young Wessels come——" suggested Diana.

"Very unlikely in this storm; besides, why should they? Yet, supposing they do, we should be on the right side of everything, because we have found them out. Now then, come along. Of course you know we are quite close to the alder creek."

Diana said it had seemed about a mile to her in the water, wrapped round by mist.

"Oh *no*, not close," she whispsred.

"Oh *yes*, a few yards," whispered Noreen in return. "My dear child, you come with me through the wood and you'll find that you came round a promontory when you were in the water. Everything looks weird in a fog—besides——" She stopped short as the lightning winked through the one little dirty window. "This is a most convenient storm," went on Noreen; "they will all be nailed to their houses. Come on, Di, we are wasting time."

Into the wood they went, Noreen leading, and in ten minutes at the outside Diana admitted she was right. For there, ahead of them, showed up the line of the next creek edged by that thick rank of alders. Once there she was able to show her friend where the launch lay, and they went down the bank to look at it, Noreen as cool as possible, and making up her energetic mind without the least hesitation.

"We now proceed to labour in the cause of right, law, and all the rest of it," said Noreen. "Look here, Di, I'll go on board—hand up parcels to you. You pile them in a heap by your side, and then I'll come up and we'll take them across as fast as we can."

Then followed a very amazing half-hour. The storm worked up to a climax, in which the wood seemed dark as twilight, and the centre of the disturbance exactly over the girls' heads. It really was rather soul-shaking, because lightning in a wood has its own effects, and they are startling!

But Diana never blenched. As for Noreen, she was as gay as though it were a summer picnic. Everything she could lift she lifted, amusing herself by guessing what was in the parcels.

"What a mercy silk is so light," she said. "I saw in the paper a few days ago that people had fetched over silk coats—*coats*, Di—and dozens of silk stockings, and scarves too. I think they were fined about a hundred and fifty pounds. Poor wretches, how—— I *say*, here comes some rain-drops as big as pats of butter! Look here, shall we get inside the motor house and keep dry? I expect all those parcels have got oiled silk inside the paper. You come inside this—why not?"

Diana protested hotly. She said she would sooner get wet.

"We truly must get these parcels into a safe place. Oh, please, Noreen," she begged.

Noreen jumped up like a cat.

"Come along—unless we sit on them to keep them dry," she laughed. "Take all you can."

Diana was only too willing. The vicinity of that launch did not please her at all. She was haunted by the fear that smugglers of the old-fashioned, desperate sort might suddenly appear. It was not a happy idea.

To and fro they went loaded with packages, and when they reached the boat-house they shoved the parcels up above the loose planks of the ceiling. The last journey was the heaviest laden, as they then carried certain deal boxes, nailed, corded, and sealed.

"'Quoth the elephant, what next?'" murmured Noreen, as she set her load down. Then she stiffened, and held up a finger for silence.

CHAPTER X

ALDER CREEK

At the moment Noreen heard the sound Diana also heard it. Just a succession of dull little bumps which the sailor girl knew for the knocking of one boat against another. Light, because both boats were afloat and moving.

From beneath the floor of the boat-house came a voice, repressed to a husky undertone—

"This Wessel's dinghy?"

"Belongs to ol' Barney down Garde way. Wessel he hired of it. My word, what a storm; regular soaker, I'm wet through. Now look here, where's Kearns? Seems to me he's a bit slow on his job."

"Kearns—who's Kearns?"

"What's the good of saying that; you know as well as I do. Ain't he the motor chap?"

"Oh, *that*! Well, you'd better do something about it, eh? Our lorry's coming along with a load soon as they can, if not sooner. They'll want to pack that launch. Wrestler will have something to say if you keep him knocking about down here. He told me to find out what was doing, and, 'cording to you, there's that launch packed with steamer goods, and this yer Kearns absent. You won't catch Wrestler handing out cash, or, for the matter of that, accepting of it, unless he sees the signal all clear. He's not one to get himself mixed up with trouble."

"Oh—p-i-g," hissed Noreen, with her lips shaping the letters.

Diana's face, which had been distinctly tense with nervous anxiety, relented into a smile. Then she took one long step close to her friend, and they put their heads together.

"W-a-it," murmured Noreen, and the other girl nodded silently.

Somehow that very short communication was a comfort, and Diana felt her strained mind ease from the nervous tension. The smile lighted her face again, and she listened to the conversation that reached their ears with a different feeling.

It was spoken very low, and was also confused at times, because both men were smoking, and interlarded their conference with growlings and mutterings.

One—the man who appeared to be the ally of Wrestler—was angry. It was plain that he expected matters to be smooth for the reception of some lorry driven by this Wrestler, and had no opinion of the skill with which the job had been managed by the steamer men and the engineer of the launch.

It was not possible to be certain whether one lorry or two were mixed up in this business, but it was pretty certain that there were the two loads Noreen had mentioned in her description. That is to say, the cargo brought by the steamer, and carried by the launch to the alder creek, and a cargo that was expected to come by lorry and be shipped by the launch to the steamer for conveyance back across the Channel.

That, as Noreen had suggested, would be too heavy for the girls to deal with.

The air was clearing—in more senses than one! Diana could see by Noreen's eyes that that energetic young woman was alive with some idea to meet the difficulty, but she was hardly prepared for the move when Noreen set a finger on her lips and noiselessly opened the door.

Diana made a signal for caution and drew back; she was inclined to shrink from any plunge into the open.

For one minute they both checked, listening involuntarily while the rain-drops hit the roof of the hut in slower and slower pats, as though it were getting tired of falling. From the woods came a soft scent of wet leaves, and the clouds were opening.

At that moment the voice of one of the men came to their ears distinctly—

"It's giving over; here, shove out. We can't stick about here all day—come on."

There followed faint noises of bumpings and irritated growls owing to the entanglement of the two boats. Then a voice below the front of the boat-house showed the men had got out.

"We never looked inside that hut," said one man.

"What for should we?" demanded the other.

"Quite so—*quite* so, my friend," murmured Noreen; then drawing close to Diana, she whispered—

"Now, come on out. Let's cut across the wood and hide and hear what they say when they find the launch is empty."

"Oh *no*!" contradicted Di. "What would be the good of that? Let's hope they will think the lorry came and took the lot, or——"

"Oh, my *dear* girl"—Noreen positively bounced as the thought struck her—"*I* know. They will think the Wessels took it all and are keeping it to sell. There will be war to the knife between Tharp Ash and the steamer men."

Diana looked troubled.

"Oh," she murmured, "poor Emily——"

Noreen shook her head.

"I don't agree about 'poor' at all. It would be the natural consequence of people doing these cheating jobs. Of course they won't trust each other. Why should they? *They* know the others tell lies to other people; well, then, why believe them? It is horrid, but natural, of course, and——"

"If you are sure of that, then, why bother to go and listen?" urged Diana. "Why not take the *Arrow* and get on board your *Gadfly*, then we can bring her round here. There is wind now—always is wind after a thunderstorm—then as soon as those men have gone back we can load up these parcels and be off."

Noreen leaned against the doorpost looking into the wet wood, frowning and considering the case from all points. Finally she decided *against* it.

"Too soon, and too obvious," she declared. "Of course we can go off to the *Gadfly* and wait on board, but we should not learn anything of their plans that way. Better find out some more now, and bring along the *Gadfly* when those men have cleared out."

Diana bowed to this decision—whatever she thought, she felt bound to let Noreen lead. She was the sailor for one thing, and, for another, there was certainly a power of leadership in this Hamilton girl difficult to withstand.

She was not sure what she wished actually, except that she did not wish to hurt poor Emily Wessel. But she was sure that the open way was to follow Noreen's lead, and she, without further argument or explanation, stepped out into the wet undergrowth and went off, picking her way like a cat on a road with puddles, while Diana did the like in the rear.

As they went, trying their hardest to be noiseless, they could hear the rhythmic jolt of the heavy oars in the rowlocks of the boat going round to alder creek.

Getting there first they chose a mass of hazel bushes on the bank just where it overhung the water, and squeezing down, well concealed, they waited to learn what should happen next.

The last thing they expected or wished was what happened, of course!

No sooner had they settled down close to the bank when the sound of footsteps advancing through the wood came to their ears: footsteps coming along the bank above, and the click of oars along the creek below.

Noreen put her lips close to Diana's ear.

"Scylla and Charybdis," she breathed, "between the devil and the deep sea, isn't it? Lots of people about, Di!"

Diana nearly giggled, there was something so irrepressible about Noreen. Nothing appeared to daunt her. She was gay as a lark. Within five minutes they realized that Job Wessel, arriving to satisfy himself about the launch, had met the two men on the boat. Moreover, they had discovered that the launch was empty, and in a minute the fact that irritation and suspicion prevailed on both sides was fairly obvious.

"What you done with the load, Wessel?" demanded the boatman, who appeared to be Pawley.

"That's for *you* to say," retorted Job. "Well, what you lookin' for, eh?"

"Same to you. You haven't made no explanation far as I can see."

That was the kind of interchange that the hidden girls listened to, and they wondered how it would end, because the two men in the boat seemed to be angry.

At intervals the suppressed voices rose hotly, then hushed again to husky whispers; but the girls gathered from the few words audible that the lorry, run by a person called Wrestler, was due that night, or next day, though neither of the men knew if the earlier one in charge of Timothy Chant had taken away the cargo from over the water or not. Job Wessel declared they had been busy on the farm, and, as he said, "however you look at it, it's not our business." He argued that "Tharp folk had agreed to keep a shut eye and take a few notes for so doing," but that was the extent of their responsibility. They had nothing to do with the "workings" of either the steamer or the lorries.

Diana glanced sideways at Noreen when these words reached their ears, glanced and smiled with a little nod of her head.

Noreen whispered into her ear, "Run with the hare, hunt with the hounds," and curled the end of her sharp little nose with a most contemptuous up-tilt.

It was plain enough that Noreen had small patience with half-hearted wrong-doers—she preferred the reckless ones!

The end of it was that Job Wessel went away growling, and the men in the boat said they should return to the steamer and tell Kearns, the driver of the launch. Both parties agreed to leave the launch where she lay, in readiness for Wrestler's van. Kearns would come off and run the *Pretty Jane* to the steamer. *Pretty Jane* was the launch.

Incidentally, inquiries must be made of Wrestler as to whether Tim Chant had unloaded the launch, and what this irregular proceeding meant.

One thing was plain: the three men were suspicious of one another, yet none of them wished to quarrel openly, because both parties depended on each other for money and success. The creeks around Tharp Ash Farm and the connivance of the Wessels were so convenient to the smugglers that they wanted to avoid a split, while the Wessels had no intention of losing the money that came so easily.

So Job Wessel went back through the copse, and the muffled click of the oars died away along alder creek.

CHAPTER XI

THEY MAKE A PLOT AND ACT

NOREEN was in her element—ready to dance with thrills and energy; yet for about five minutes she sat tight, so to speak, impressing on Diana the full force of the adventure thrust upon them.

" First, we get the *Gadfly* and load her up with the goods in the boat-house, because, my dear girl, you've got to realize that the quicker that cargo is shifted aboard our boat the better it will be for our scheme."

Diana nodded, her eyes fixed on the running water at the foot of the bank.

" And then we take it all to Crow's Market ? " she suggested.

" Oh no, we don't," said Noreen, " not *then*."

Diana glanced up quickly and caught a positive flash of excitement in the blue-green eyes watching her.

" But I thought——" she began.

" Don't *think*—we must *do* as hard as we can work till those goods are shifted. Then I run the *Gadfly*—well—probably to Garde, to her moorings. You go home—to Tharp Farm I mean—and sleep as long as you choose."

There was a pause while Noreen frowned to herself, her lips pursed up into a whistle—then suddenly she added—

"Wrestler's lorry comes *to-morrow*, loads up this *Pretty Jane*, and goes away. Now I wonder——"

Noreen stopped whispering and gazed at Diana with her head on one side for half a minute.

"Wonder! What?" The other girl was puzzled.

"I was wondering if by any chance you could keep the Wessels out of the way," answered Noreen.

"Out of whose way, or what way?"

This was a very natural question, but it was not answered, because Noreen simply said, "I must think about that," which conveyed no meaning whatever.

However, just at that moment there really was no time for explaining "thoughts," unless they were severely practical. The presence of that mass of packages shut out imagination; there was no room for anything now but just busy lifting and hard work.

The two went off at once, through the wood to the boat-house: looked at the "cargo" to see if it was safe, shipped on board the *Arrow*, which was floating beneath the little wooden erection, and went on their way to fetch the *Gadfly* within reasonable distance for the work that was to come.

There was wind and to spare now. The *Gadfly* swung at her moorings full of life as though she wanted to take advantage of the puffs of wind and buffeting gusts that had arisen as wind does after thunder. All the world was uneasy. The water washed up under the wet banks, the trees bent and bowed, sending showers of drops pattering on the water. But it mattered not at all to Noreen, because the one thing she most wanted was secure. No one was about. The shores were deserted in their damp stickiness, and plainly the steamer's dinghy had gone back to that vessel for the men to get dry and wait in comfort till either of the lorries should turn up—next day—and give them something to do.

As they smoked in the cabin they told their mates that it was no good trusting the Wessel family. Pawley had more than a suspicion that the young men had "double-crossed" the steamer gang.

So they talked more and more, but did nothing else, fortunately for the two girls, who dropped anchor within the curve of that channel up to Midbrake, safe, silent, out of sight, and from there began the arduous work of making journeys to and fro between the resting *Gadfly* and the boat-house.

One might think it would have been easier to anchor at the mouth of that creek, but Noreen dismissed the idea without argument, as far too obvious. Boats from the steamer to the alder creek would never come round by the Midbrake channel—that would be quite a mile and a half out of the way! The little cutter was as safe in her anchorage as anywhere in the waters, and Noreen meant to sleep on board. She had told her mother not to worry.

"I shall lock myself in with the silk stockings and the scent," she said. "If I can't sleep I might try some of them on to pass the time."

They were about an hour transferring all the parcels, and when it was done Diana thought her arms would never be any use again. But she said it was splendid exercise, which was, of course, quite true. There was intense satisfaction in clearing the whole thing out, and when they had settled the last load neatly within the *Gadfly's* long cabin, Noreen made cocoa, and they both refreshed themselves with that and excellent potted-meat sandwiches made by Mrs. Hamilton's Irish servant.

"Have I eaten up your night meal?" asked Diana, stretching out luxuriously on the cushions of the seat.

"If you have I can satisfy myself with good deeds," answered Noreen from the bunk. "Virtue is its own reward, my dear; just think of all we have done."

"Oh, I do, and my brain simply swells with admiration. But, Noreen, I want to know what happens next. You had something on your mind—what was it? Now we are not in a racing hurry and this job is done—honestly, I want to know what next."

And Noreen, with her feet stretched out and her tired arms resting supine, told her amazed friend what she was going to do.

"Stars and stripes!" gasped Diana, as she tried to visualize the whole proceeding, "then you won't want the *Arrow*?"

"Oh no, I shall swim and walk. Having no dinghy at all disarms suspicion; people naturally think you *can't* get ashore. If you have a boat alongside, of course, they know there is some one on board too."

Finally Diana told her she was a most surprising person.

"Oh, I know," allowed Noreen. "Mother says I take after Dad. He *is* astonishing, if you like—always inventing things. I wish I could. I only do what happens to get in the way—like this."

"And I'm no earthly use!" despaired Diana, moving restlessly. "Here will you be doing amazing things, and I just loafing about at Tharp Ash, feeling sick because I can't help."

"Hum—hum," murmured her friend. "Of course, if you could think——" And sitting up with her arms around her bent-up knees, she propounded a plan to Diana, who stared at her, leaning on one elbow—stared amazed, and with her mind wandering off into conjecture. If she *could*!

"Mind you," said Noreen tolerantly, "I don't say you could think of anything, but one has only to consider the notion all round to realize what a help it would be if——"

"Oh! I *do*," agreed Diana. "And, naturally, if I were stopping out there by the boat-house I should hear what was going on."

"But remember this, my dear," concluded Noreen, "don't *risk* anything. I can always invent plans—they positively bubble in my brain. I would not have you risk things for worlds when you are coming out of measles and all that. If you see a reasonable plan—well and good; but whatever happens I shall get through this—you'll see."

There was something about the *Gadfly's* skipper that acted like a tonic on Diana: she was so undaunted in her faith and courage, never doubting success, never fearing failure. Diana, on the contrary, though brave enough in emergency, was timid about facing difficulties, and in this queer maze of adventure she was inclined to fear pitfalls. However, Noreen had waked her up into a new mood, and she was keen now to meet her friend half-way, therefore she dropped into the dinghy, grasped the sculls, and went off inspired with zeal to think and act

Diana often thought afterwards that that was the queerest evening she had spent in her life. She tied up the *Arrow*, went in to supper, and put off Emily's questions with talk about the storm.

Yes, she had been to Garde as she said. Yes, she had seen Miss Hamilton and had been on board the *Gadfly*—and so on. Everything fitted neatly, yet nothing she said told the actual story of the afternoon.

She went to bed and to sleep, soundly, yet every hour she was listening for the faint noise of a motor, and early in the morning she awoke to realize that the day was rather grey and windy, with swaying trees, and a feeling of disturbance in the air.

" You won't go out, missie ? " suggested Mrs. Wessel, who seemed to have rather a restless eye that morning.

" Oh, I expect I shall go and bathe," said Diana, looking out of the window. " When is high tide, Emily ? "

Mrs. Wessel said she " opined " that the tide would be high about four o'clock in the afternoon. " Top of the flood, Miss Di, so far as I understand. That's to say I believe it will be running out after four. There'll be plenty of water up all middle day, the wind will be drivin' of it in."

Mrs. Wessel had a fixed idea that the wind had a lot to do with high or low tides ! Diana said nothing—she was calculating on Noreen's probable movements.

" Oh, well," she said, " I shall bathe sometime, and, of course, I might go out a bit in the dinghy. I love boats Emily. It was kind of the farmer to get that for me."

She did as she said she would in the bathing line went down to the hut, and, presently, with infinite caution, went across to look at the hidden launch. In so doing she grasped what she had not realized—that as the launch was on the *mud* under the alders, no one could get it off till the tide rose. Also, when it was loaded with the heavy cases of tea and tobacco, it would be still heavier!

She had only got to use her own common sense in calculating, to understand when that launch could be moved.

"And, of course," thought Diana, "Noreen will know exactly."

She was having dinner in her little sitting-room when she heard the noise of a motor. As Mrs. Wessel came in with her pudding, she asked—

"A motor, Emily; quite exciting in this quiet place. Who is it?"

"Only something for the master, missie," answered Emily, turning a dull red under her sallow skin. "Or," she added, with some truth this time, "there's folks uses them creeks for carrying to an' fro. None of Tharp business."

And Diana suddenly felt sorry for the poor woman. There was bitterness in her voice, or so it seemed. After all, Emily was not the "power behind the wheel" in this case.

Diana was so excited that she could hardly eat that pudding, and after dinner she sat in the armchair with the broken spring, calculating times and picturing to herself how Noreen was getting ready for her supreme attack on the enemy.

Presently, unable to bear inaction any longer, she got up and fetched her hat and shoes. Then Mrs. Wessel came in.

"I'm going out in the *Arrow*, Emily," she said, and immediately understood that this was an anxiety, and that Emily wanted her to stop indoors. Why?

"Now don't you, Miss Di. It might be nice and fine after tea—go out then."

The tide calculation sped through Diana's mind again: high water, between three and four probably, and the launch fetched away, no doubt! Till then she was to keep out of the way.

Noreen would know the exact time, and *before* these men came she would act!

What Diana said was—

"Probably it will be quite fine directly. 'Ten and two tell what the day will do.' I came here to be out-of-doors, Emily," and she laughed. She was feeling excited and rather out of herself.

At two o'clock she went to the boat-house, found everything as usual, and suddenly became inspired by a desire to look for blackberries in the wood. She wandered up through the undergrowth, watchful eyes on the line of the alder creek. Sounds of subdued talking came to her ears, and she saw the figures of the two Wessel youths standing above the bank with another man. Then she made out the shape of the lorry, and realized that another man was replacing a tarpaulin over the back part of it.

If the tarpaulin was being replaced the load had certainly been removed, and while she stood hesitating she noted the man who had been speaking to young Wessel make a sign of farewell with one hand and jump up into the covered part in the front of the lorry.

There was a throbbing sound, and then, with wonderfully little noise considering, the little vehicle started and went off, gathering speed as it disappeared along the cart track up towards the road.

The two Wessel men remained on the bank, staring

down into the alder brake at the place where the loaded launch should be.

Diana wondered if they had been asking Mr. Wrestler and his mate what had happened to the first cargo! It was all so strange and so amazing.

Then she remembered in a rush that now was her moment to help Noreen.

CHAPTER XII

THEY WIN THE GAME

ONE thing was certain: Diana had not actually planned out her action, and yet in that exciting moment she behaved as though every action had been rehearsed. She knew that the one thing that mattered was to get the Wessel youths away from the alder creek and the neighbourhood of the launch at whatever cost to herself.

Silently she sped back to the boat-house on the Tharp Ash creek, jumped into the dinghy, pointed the little boat down to the entrance of the creek, where it was wider and the water deeper. Then she deliberately pitched one oar overboard, sending it out as far as she could. After that she gazed round carefully to see that no one was in sight, and, having assured herself of complete isolation, she suddenly *screamed*.

Shriek after shriek proceeded from Diana with as much realistic terror as she could put into the noise. While she did it, she jumped on to the gunwale of the boat, upset it completely, and disappeared under the Blacksand water with a mighty splash.

As soon as she came up she screamed again—rather a choked scream this time, and with all her weight grabbed on to the *Arrow*, which was by this time upside down, with the thwarts and the bottom boards floating gaily away on the rising tide.

Diana shook her head free of water, struck out with her feet to keep in deeper water, and screamed again in a thoroughly energetic manner.

The result was better than her wildest hopes, because the two Wessel sons came crashing through the copse towards the boat-house side of the creek, while poor Mrs. Emily appeared from the direction of the house, making her wild way along the other side, screaming for help as she came, and followed by the one old dog, that for once left the kitchen fireside to bark in her wake.

"Better than one could have hoped, even," thought Diana, as she noted the distracted members of the Wessel family arriving in force, and she proceeded to colour the picture with deft touches.

It is commonly supposed that people with marked black eyebrows and expressive dark eyes are actresses and actors by nature. That may or may not be so, but it is certain that Diana had a gift that way, and in this exciting moment she made use of her talent, for she let go the boat's keel, threw up her arms, and with one gurgling shriek allowed herself to disappear backwards.

The cries of poor Emily were at this awful moment heartrending. The dog barked till it coughed, plunged into the water, and swam out towards the boat.

The younger Wessel, Stanley, could swim a little. Job, like so many of his kind, could not. However, they both went into the water, finding, as they waded out, that the creek was not deep enough to drown them, whatever it might do to Diana. This knowledge, of course, was heartening. They two and Rover, the dog, all reached the overturned boat at the same time, to find Diana holding on with her eyes shut.

" You're all right, missie," encouraged Job, and then at the top of his voice he bawled to Emily—

" She's all right, missus."

Diana wanted to laugh, but turned it into a cough. At this moment Rover barged into the party and tried to lick all their faces. Probably he felt they needed encouragement.

Just at that moment Diana heard the rattling chug-chug of the motor launch, and glancing swiftly at Stanley, saw him in turn look at his brother.

It was momentary, but Diana knew that Noreen was making her move, and undoubtedly the two Wessels thought Kearns, the motor man, had fetched the cargo.

They wanted to distract attention from *his* work, and Diana was willing enough on her side to keep all eyes on the spot !

The result was a good deal of fuss and splashing, as she, the boat, and the two rescuers propelled themselves to the bank on which stood Emily Wessel making miserable noises.

Rover got out first and shook himself into a perfect wheel of sparks.

Diana said, " Oh dear, I am so wet," which was not a brilliant remark, because it was obvious.

Mrs. Wessel said, " Whatever will your mamma say, Miss Di ? Stanley, you go back in and fetch them oars, or we'll have Mr. Barney charging for them."

Job said, " Don't you worry, Missus ; tide's flowing, them things will come ashore right enough." He was emptying the water out of the boat, and listening all the time to the busy chug-chug of a motor launch receding in the distance.

"Gone up towards Midbrake," thought Diana, thrilling with excitement and joy. So she had helped Noreen after all!

In the excess of her satisfaction she beamed on Mrs. Wessel and begged her not to worry.

"I'm perfectly all right, Emily," she reasoned; "only wet. I'll run to the house and change."

Then she thanked the rescuers warmly.

"It won't make the *least* difference to my going out in the boat," she said. "Of course, I can swim a bit, only one's clothes do weigh so heavy. Now, please do go in and have dry things."

Everybody went in, leaving the *Arrow* tied up with thwarts, bottom boards, and sculls complete.

Rover went in and shook himself again thoroughly all over the clean door-step. Everybody drank hot tea. Diana sat before a fresh-lighted fire in her own little sitting-room, with dry clothes, and a sense of well-being all over her. She had buttered toast for tea, and was more hungry than she had been since she arrived at Tharp Ash.

"To look at you, missie, I'd say you was in for a feverish attack," remarked Emily gloomily.

Diana said she was feeling well.

"You see, all this makes life much more interesting," she explained.

"Ah, that's the fever on you," said Emily.

"Anyway, it won't make the least difference to my going out in the boat or bathing, or anything," Diana told her with a firmness that Mrs. Wessel put down to delirium. " I'm not going to have my nice time here spoilt by just upsetting a boat. Emily, you make most glorious toast. It is so kind of you."

Emily went away softened.

Late that evening, when the tide was low and mudbanks showing all along the Blacksand waters, Diana heard voices in the kitchen, voices that seemed to be argumentative, not to say angry, and she wondered very much whether Kearns, the motor man, or one of the others whose names she could not be sure of, had come up to Tharp Ash to make " railing accusations " against the Wessel sons, who really and truly seemed to be fairly blameless.

Diana herself did not go out again. She thought it over, and decided to wait for some sign from Noreen and the *Gadfly*. It appeared wiser not to rouse Emily's suspicions just now while she knew the tide would be at the lowest ebb at somewhere near nine o'clock, so that Noreen might be tied up in her channel till the flow covered all that dangerous mud world in the faint grey dawn.

It did not seem fair to frighten poor old Emily again. She would wait.

Having made up her mind she slept well. Having slept undisturbed by the wind over the waters, Diana waked up full of energy before seven o'clock. She lay still counting on her fingers the hours when tides would be up or down, and having counted, decided that unless she went down to the creek at once, there would be small chance of getting at Noreen till the afternoon, because the mudbanks would prevail.

She dressed herself swiftly, and without attempting concealment, went boldly out by the front door. She took the way to the boat-house round by the farm sheds and the wood, and to her joy found the dinghy tied to the piles, dry and respectable.

She ran along to the shore, and saw, floating in the shallow water of the ebbing channel, the *Gadfly*, her dark-red mainsail heaped on the deck, just lashed carelessly to keep it in place, but not stowed, her jib in the same case—a look about her as though she had come through stiff work and was just resting.

Diana gazed with absorbed interest, then she sped back to the boat-house, crept down the bank and boarded the dinghy, pushed her out into the low channel, and went off with vigorous strokes.

In a few minutes she slid alongside the little cutter. Then she whistled. As there was no answer she climbed on board, made fast her boat, and looked down into the cabin.

There was Noreen sound asleep in her own bunk—the cabin tidy as always, no trace whatever of that very unlawful cargo.

Diana gazed, taking in the appearance of the charming little saloon. She thought, " Was it real, or else just a wild dream ? "

Then she saw that Noreen was looking at her.

" Hallo ! " said Noreen, " that stunt of yours was simply top-hole, my dear. I do assure you your yells pierced my vitals. I felt a murderess going off with the launch and leaving you to a watery grave."

Diana jumped down into the cuddy.

" I had three rescuers," she said, " let alone dear old Emily, who made hot toast for me with tears trickling down her cheeks—two Wessel sons and fat Rover, who enjoyed it all awfully. I was all right.

But truly, Noreen, I'm on thorns to hear what happened to you. I was so sick with envy when I thought of your glorious adventure that I could hardly bear to go to bed. However, I did stop, as you know, because of Emily. But tell me. Can I sit down here and you tell? Did you have a fearfully exciting time?"

Noreen laughed.

"Quite. Oh, *quite*," she murmured. "I'll try and put it in few words. I was waiting near the launch, as you can guess. I saw them load. When you yelled and the Wessel boys ran, I climbed in, set the engine going, and had all my work cut out to start, because she was a bit stuck. However, we went down the channel to Midbrake in great style. I'd half a mind to get on to Crow's Market, but didn't, because I was keen to sail the *Gadfly* out of danger. I just went round to old Walduck's place, ran into the creek there, and rushed the launch up on *his* mud. Safe as Westminster Hall, naturally. He came along and I explained in condensed language. He grunted and lashed up the launch to a few trees. Said he would hold her till the Customs' men came. He really was rather an angel, old thing, because he gave me about half a gallon of hot tea and a foot of cake—divine cake, too. Then he rowed me back to the *Gadfly*—you know his boat. By that time your body had been carried indoors and the coast was clear, so I set sail and went off, feeling very hearty."

Here Noreen sat up and ran her fingers through her hair.

"I did have rather a time, Diana," she went on. "There was a wind and clouds, moon sulky, tides fiendish! Fortunately I know Crow's Market all right, and nothing interfered—I mean no humans. Tide was very low when I got there, of course, but it wasn't dark, and there were plenty of people about on the quays. I picked up moorings and an old Johnny to keep guard on board while I hunted up Authorities. Offices were shut, but I found where the man lived, and very soon a stream of tin hats came trotting down like ants after a jam jar. I do assure you I made things hum——"

"You would," murmured Diana, rapturously admiring.

"They sent off a powerful launch to pick off the one at Midbrake, and then unloaded the *Gadfly*. My word, Di, I *was* glad to see all those parcels go, they were so frightfully in the way, weren't they?"

Diana nodded.

"Think of all those silk stockings," she murmured.

"I don't. They are no good to me. I'd sooner have the eau-de-Cologne for Mum. However, they got the lot. And as soon as the *Gadfly* and I felt clear and comfy we came off."

"What, at once? Noreen, you really *are*——"

"My good child—it was a fair wind, strongish, a flowing tide—great. We came back, I do assure you, like racing in a regatta, and I didn't mind letting her rip, as the tide was rising fast. We took less than one hour, no trouble. I anchored, had cocoa, and went to sleep—absolutely *shining* with virtue. The tin hats are busy as bees over the affair. Steamer, launch, and lorries will all have to pay up big fines."

"Noreen," broke in Diana anxiously, "the farm people won't get hurt, will they? *Poor* Emily! Besides, the Wessel sons were awfully kind when they thought I was drowning—*poor* things!"

"They deserve rather a smack, my dear girl," answered Noreen, lying down again. "*I* don't want to hurt them, of course, but they have been jolly dishonest for months. It will be a case of 'let this be a warning to you' kind of thing, and no more, probably, because I never mentioned their names. The launch was in Alder Creek, too. There will not be evidence against old Job, as far as I know. And so that's that, my child—a most surprising adventure—quite worth living for."

There was a pause, then Noreen sat up again and stared at her friend with an odd expression in her keen eyes.

"*What?*" murmured Diana, in an anxious tone.

"Something—rather thrilling. I say, Di, should you be surprised if I told you that *we*—you and I—will probably get a reward?"

"Reward! Oh!" Diana visualized five pounds, with vague conclusions about boots for winter.

"Yes," went on Noreen, an odd little flicker of feeling passing across her face. "It's something pretty big by what the boss man suggested. Oh, *quite* big—some hundreds of pounds—for catching out the whole machinery *and* the cargoes. Considering how hard my father works, for nothing, really, and your father too, well, I must say I think it's something to rejoice about. Personally, I give the idea unlimited praise. What do you say?"

"Oh, but I did *nothing*," cried Diana, her eyes filling with tears.

"Of course you did—witness your shrieks when you

were drowning," retorted Noreen. "And now look here, you'd better go home and soothe Emily while I dress and eat, and clean up my *Gadfly*. Then you come back and sail up to Garde with me, and we'll break the news to my angelic parents. They really do deserve a treat sometimes, bless them."

. . . .

That is the actual end of that amazing adventure, when Noreen Hamilton snuffed out the smugglers in Blacksand waters with Diana Lindsay to help her.

It was true about the reward, too. But that was a part of the story neither of the girls dwelt upon very much. The adventure was a joyous beginning of great times on the *Gadfly* later.

THE END

PRINTED IN GREAT BRITAIN AT
THE PRESS OF THE PUBLISHERS

ESTABLISHED 1798

T. NELSON
& SONS, LTD.
PRINTERS AND
PUBLISHERS